OPERATION FIREWORKS

OPERATION ROMANCE BOOK 3

ELIZABETH MADDREY

Scripture quoted by permission. Quotations designated (NIV) are from THE HOLY BIBLE: NEW INTERNATIONAL VERSION®. NIV®. Copyright © 1973, 1978, 1984 by Biblica. All rights reserved worldwide.

Cover design by Elizabeth Maddrey.

Cover art photos ©iStockphoto.com/heather_mcgrath, ©iStockphoto.-com/Tomwang112 used by permission.

Published in the United States of America by Elizabeth Maddrey. www.ElizabethMaddrey.com

For Tim
Because even after all these years
We still have plenty of fireworks.

1

J ake McGill grabbed the canvas duffel from the back of
his truck and slung it over his shoulder. Three weeks off.
Intelligence Associates would be fine without him.
Honestly, they'd probably be fine without him if he took
six weeks off. But what would he do with himself for that long?
As it was, he was spending his vacation in the mountainous
southern tip of Virginia working at a camp. He shook his head.
He'd given Gabe such a hard time about using his vacation to
run the Christmas light fundraiser for Operation Mistletoe.
And he'd teased Rick about going in to the office when he was
back in the States at the start of the year on vacation. and here
he was, doing effectively the same thing. None of them knew
how to relax.

At least Gabe and Rick had each managed to snare a
woman in the process. That wasn't likely to happen here. The
camp was primarily staffed by married couples or college
students. The camp director had sounded suspicious when
Jake applied for the trail guide and riflery instructor position.
Thankfully, his references had checked out and she'd come
around. The need for a counselor must've outweighed the

desire for that person to be married. That and the fact that he was qualified to do the Fourth of July fireworks. Maybe that's what pushed her over the edge to take him on. There couldn't be that many people willing to come for just room and board.

Jake shrugged and trudged up the path from the parking area to the main lodge to check in. It wasn't as if he'd be sleeping in the same cabin with a group of kids. No. Corralling the campers who wanted to hike and learn survival skills or how to shoot a BB gun was one thing. But to herd them from place to place, eat with them, do nightly devotions? That was not his scene. He'd get to spend time in the mountains, teach the kids a few things, and send them back to their cabins at night, leaving him with plenty of time to read and relax.

Jake pulled open the screen door, wincing as the hinges screamed in protest, and stepped into the sprawling, high-ceilinged room. Three ping pong tables lined one long wall on the far side, couches that had seen better days were clustered in groupings around low tables in the rest of the room. If this was all they had to offer for recreation on rainy days, he'd keep his fingers crossed that the weather stayed clear. He dropped his duffel and tucked his hands in his pockets as he looked around.

Aha. A door tucked in the corner had peeling letters that labeled it the office. He crossed the space and rapped on it.

"Come in."

His eyebrows lifted. The voice was younger than he'd antici-pated. The woman he'd dealt with as he set up his time here had come across as older. And mean. Jake pushed open the door and froze. It definitely wasn't the mannish retired gym teacher he'd constructed in his mind. The woman behind the desk was striking. She was probably about his age, though her luminous skin would make younger women envious. Jake cleared his throat. "Morning. Jake McGill, checking in."

"Mr. McGill. Have a seat and I'll be right with you." She

didn't look up, but continued tapping away at the laptop on her desk.

All right. At least the view was nice. Jake lowered himself into the metal folding chair that sat opposite the desk and propped an ankle on his knee. What was her name? The nameplate on the desk simply said CAMP DIRECTOR. Did they go through so many that it wasn't cost effective to personalize? Her strawberry blonde ponytail swung slightly as she hammered the keys. He didn't envy whoever was on the receiving end of her electronic diatribe.

Finally, she looked up, her blue eyes piercing. "Mr. McGill, I'm Deborah Magarry. Mrs. Beech, the usual camp director, was taken ill last week and her doctors have advised her to take the rest of the summer off. I'll be filling in until they can find a permanent replacement."

That explained it, then. He grinned. "Pleasure to meet you."

"We'll see. I've been going over all the paperwork for counselors prior to the campers arriving tomorrow morning. It turns out that there were anomalies in several of the applications that should have resulted in a firm, but polite, refusal. Thus, we're all going to have to pitch in and pick up the extra work as needed." Deborah offered a tight smile. "You'll be in cabin seven. Here's the folder with information on your charges. You'll be responsible for ensuring that they keep the room tidy, as much as seven and eight year old boys are capable of doing so. You'll also need to have an evening devotional each night before lights out. I've put a list of suggestions for topics in the folder as well. Your schedule is the very top sheet. See that each group gets to their activities on time, without losing any of the kids along the way. And be back to pick them up at the end of the session. The other counselors know you're doing double duty, so they'll wait with their campers until you arrive at the hiking trail head or the shooting range. Any questions?"

Only about a thousand. Jake shook his head. "I'm not...a cabin of kids? That's not what I signed up for."

Her lips thinned. "I'm aware of that. I also believe I mentioned that this is necessary. Unless, of course, you'd like to call those eight families and explain why they shouldn't come drop their kids off tomorrow?"

It was tempting. He liked kids well enough. But mostly when you had a concrete plan to acquire them, teach them something, and get them back to their parents. That's how the youth group had roped him into helping Gabe and it was going all right. Jake mostly brought snacks and hung out with the guys. But those were high school kids. Not—what grade were eight year olds anyway? "No. That won't be necessary. Cabin seven, you said?"

For the briefest moment, Deborah's smile reached her eyes. "There's a map on the back of your schedule. You've got tonight to get settled. Dinner is at five in the dining hall and then we have leader devotions and a team building exercise followed by a campfire."

"When am I supposed to settle in again?"

Deborah glanced at the slim gold watch on her wrist. "You have nearly seven hours before dinner. Surely that's plenty? Though you'll probably want to check the supplies for the shooting range. Let me get you the key."

JAKE LOCKED the shed and slipped the key into his pocket. They had BB guns and BBs, paper targets, and sandbags. Though he wasn't sure he'd let them use the sandbags. At some point you had to learn to steady the barrel on your own, you couldn't always count on having a convenient prop nearby. Why not learn right from the get-go?

Cabin seven. He shook his head. He'd stopped long enough

to drop his duffel bag inside the door before angling off to the range. With that settled, it was time to go back and see what his sleeping arrangements were going to be for the next three weeks.

"Everything okay with the BB guns?" Deborah strode up alongside him as he turned onto the main path that led to the cabins. Her long, tanned legs easily matching his pace.

"Looks fine. The kids'll have fun." He shrugged. Did she ever smile?

"And the cabin?"

"I didn't really look around. I'm headed there now. I expect it's about what I remember from camp as a kid though."

She nodded. "Maybe so. Though you do have a separate bedroom. So you don't have to go to bed at lights out. Of course, after a week, you may want to."

Jake chuckled.

"I'm serious, Mr. McGill. Get the rest you need. You're no good to the campers if you're exhausted."

"Jake. You can call me Jake."

"I can, but I have no intention of doing so."

He frowned. "I'm not making the kids call me Mr. McGill, but if you want to be the only person at the camp who doesn't use my name, that's your prerogative."

She stopped, crossing her arms. "We prefer to have a modicum of formality at this camp, Mr. McGill. You're not to be one of the kids, you're their counselor, a mentor, and role model."

Modicum of formality? He couldn't stop the smile. Anger did amazing things to the light in her eyes. Did she have any idea how pretty she was? "Look, Debbie."

"Ms. Magarry."

"Seriously?"

She inclined her head.

"Fine. Miz Magarry." He drawled the name, drawing out the

z sound at the end of Ms. Did that mean she wasn't married? His gaze flicked to her left hand but he couldn't get a good view of her ring finger. "I can be all those things and still have the kids call me Jake. In fact, I'd be willing to bet I'll do an even better job if they're not treating me like I'm their school principal."

"I won't have chaos at this camp. Mrs. Beech has entrusted this session to my care and I intend to see that things are run efficiently and with decorum."

"It's a kid's camp. I'm pretty sure decorum is the last thing they want for their time away from home over the summer. They're supposed to be running around, whooping, and playing pranks on the girls' cabins. That's a rite of passage."

"What the children want is not my concern. Parents are entrusting us with their kids. I intend to see that we don't break their trust."

"And calling me Jake does that how?"

She sighed and her toe began to tap. "By instilling a sense of entitlement and lack of respect for their elders."

Jake opened his mouth, thought better of the words on the tip of his tongue, and closed it, taking a deep breath instead. "What if we met half-way? They can call me Mr. Jake. We're far enough south, that ought to work, right?"

Deborah pressed her lips together and held his gaze for several heartbeats. "Fine. I can accept that compromise."

He grinned. That wasn't so hard. Maybe she could relax a little, after all. Sure, running a camp was probably a lot of work, but he was willing to bet if she loosened up a little she could do a better job and maybe even enjoy herself in the meantime. "So, is this your first year as well?"

She shook her head. "I've been bringing my son since he was five. He's a counselor-in-training this year and one of the lifeguards at the pool."

That didn't seem possible. CITs had to be fifteen, he'd seen that on the website. She must be older than he first thought. "You must be proud."

"I am. He's a good boy." She cleared her throat. "If you'll excuse me, I have details to see to before tonight."

Jake's eyebrows lifted as she walked away, turning down the path that, if memory served, led to the girls' cabins and, after that, the dining hall. He liked a woman with fire. And she was certainly easy on the eyes. Still, that many prickles would be an awful lot of work.

Good thing he was always up for a challenge.

2

Deb seethed as she strode past the girls' cabins. Jake McGill. She'd always known God had a sense of humor, but Jake? Really? How did he not recognize her? Sure, it'd been fifteen years, and they'd been kids, barely into their second year of high school. And it wasn't as if they'd dated. They hadn't even really been in the same crowd, though she'd had a major crush on him from the moment she first saw him. Which was why she'd wrangled an invitation to that party. They'd talked then. And more than talked, even though he'd been drinking. And then her father had gotten transferred right before spring break, so instead of spending a week at the beach with her youth group, she'd added yet another move to her resume.

She sighed. When she'd told her mom she was pregnant two months later, school was just getting out. So no one had to know why they'd decided to homeschool for her junior and senior years. Her parents had pushed—hard—for her to give up the baby. And she nearly had. In the end, she hadn't been able to make herself do it. Once her parents got over their heartbreak, they'd helped as much as they could. Sean won them over. Half the time Deb was convinced they loved him more than they'd ever loved her.

She stopped outside the dining hall and took a deep breath. Jake McGill. If he didn't recognize her, she wasn't going to point it out. In fact, she'd have as little to do with him as she could. He was only here for three weeks. Once the fireworks were over, he'd get back to his life, and she could forget about him. Again.

Her heart twinged. Deb straightened her spine. She didn't need a man. Hadn't for the last fifteen years. And she wasn't still infatuated with Jake.

That would be ridiculous.

~

"HEY, MOM." Sean slung his arm around Deb's shoulders and squeezed.

"Hi, baby. You're finished at the pool?" Deb glanced at her watch. He'd gotten done early. "Did you get your cabin assignment yet?"

"Not much to do at the pool. All the lifeguards have been coming here for years, like me. Dude in charge..."

Deb cleared her throat and arched an eyebrow.

Red crept up Sean's neck. "Sorry, Mr. Langsdon, has the schedule put together already, so he just made sure we knew where everything was, double checked that our certifications were up to date, and we're set. I'm on from ten to lunch, then again from four to dinner each day."

"That's not very many hours. Just three?"

He shrugged.

"Do you want me to say something to him?"

Sean shook his head. "Naw, Mom. It's fine. There's lots to

do. Heard they actually found someone to do rifles this year. I thought I might stop by and see if there was an extra spot now and then."

Deb bit her tongue. Rifles had been Sean's favorite from the time he was old enough to shoot. Not having an instructor the past two years had been a major disappointment. She studied his face. You could see Jake in him, if you knew where to look. Would Jake? What was she supposed to do?

"What? You said enrollment's down this year. But I won't kick campers out, if that's what you're worried about."

"No." She patted his shoulder. "No, of course not. I'm sorry, my mind is so full of things to organize with Mrs. Beech gone. I'm sure it'll be fine."

He grinned, the neon rubber bands on his braces making it look like he had a mouthful of candy. Why had she ever agreed to that? Right, because rubber bands for braces were a small thing with no eternal value. How had her mother lived through the teen years? So far, at least, Sean showed little interest in girls. Maybe that would continue for another six years?

"Who's your counselor-in-training lead? Do you know yet?"

"I figured you'd tell me. You're in charge, aren't you?"

She laughed. "That list is probably buried on the desk in the office somewhere. I was just going to double check that everything was set for the bonfire tonight and then head back there. If you want to tag along, I can put you in charge of passing out assignments to the other counselor trainees."

"Sure. Maybe Cookie will give me a snack. I heard she's making brownies for dessert tonight."

"Bottomless pit. Come on, let's go find out."

~

DEB LEANED against one of the logs surrounding the bonfire and stretched out her legs. The chaplain had asked to lead this portion of the evening's program, which let her completely off the hook. She could relax and observe. Sean was sitting across the circle with the other two Counselors-in-Training. Both girls. Did boys not go to camp anymore once they hit high school? The whole camp was girl-heavy. There were only two cabins for boys this session. At least the other counselor was a returning one, so he'd ended up being in charge of Sean's CIT time. Not Jake.

Her gaze locked with Jake's as she looked around the fire. Her muscles clenched. What right did he have to show up here looking like that? The boyish charm he'd exuded in high school had deepened, matured. And he was built now, too. So unfair. Why did her traitorous heart do a little flip when he looked her way? She nodded briskly and forced herself to look into the flames. When Sean was on his own, she could start thinking about finding someone for herself. But right now, he was her priority. Had to be. She wasn't going to subject him to the ups and downs of a dating mom simply to avoid the occasional bout of loneliness. The handful of single-parent friends she had all dated, and thought she was an idiot for not doing so. But this was something she'd settled on after lots of prayer. So she'd see it through. Unless God told her otherwise.

"This is a smaller group than usual for our first session." The chaplain, Gary, looked over at Deb and raised his eyebrows. "Is enrollment really down that much?"

Deb sighed. "It's lower, certainly. But we do have ten to a cabin this summer, rather than our usual eight. The next session is completely full, however. I suspect we can blame the heavy snow in some parts of the state, which extended the school year. If kids didn't get out until this week, most parents aren't going to immediately ship them off to camp. Before Mrs. Beech took ill, she'd been talking with the camp owners about the possibility of a third session."

Gary grinned and strummed a chord on his guitar. He fiddled with the tuners and strummed again. "That's excellent. Thanks, Deb."

She frowned but didn't correct him. She'd have a word with him in private and remind him that Ms. Magarry was the appropriate form of address now that she was the camp director. It didn't matter that they'd been counselors together for years. Her new position came with more responsibility and she couldn't be fraternizing with the staff.

Gary strummed the guitar again, moving from random chords to the opening to the song that would be the theme for the three week session. "Now, let's spend some time together worshipping God. Since one of the primary purposes behind this camp is discipleship—and evangelism, for all these are mainly church kids—it's critical that everyone here be strengthening their own walk with Jesus. 'Cause when God starts to move, and He will, I've seen it happen every year, Satan tries to block everyone's spiritual progress. I'm here for you all as well as the campers, so never hesitate to come by for a chat."

Deb sang along, her gaze traveling over the faces of the counselors and other staff who would make these three weeks something special for the just under eighty campers who were registered and would begin arriving tomorrow. Six cabins of girls. Two of boys. The ages were spread out, too. Boys ranged from seven to thirteen. The girls from seven to fourteen. The girls, at least, had enough in each age bracket to lump them together in cabins by grade. The boys were a mish-mash. Hopefully, that wouldn't cause problems.

She watched Sean and smiled. He sang with such abandon. She hadn't been anywhere near as interested in God at his age. Obviously, since she'd ended up pregnant. Deb shook her head. She wouldn't go back and change it for the world, not if it meant she'd lose out on Sean. But she wished there was a way to have spared her parents the heartbreak. They'd both aged dramatically that first year.

Now she was doing everything she could to make them proud. And maybe finally she'd feel the forgiveness they said she had.

3

Jake tucked the camp t-shirt into his khaki shorts and sat on the edge of the bed to put on his hiking boots. Ten campers arriving after breakfast. If his stomach kept twisting like it was now, he'd better stick with a light morning meal. Visiting the nurse's cabin before lunch was hardly the way to win the respect of his campers. He flipped through the folder one final time. He'd spent time last night, after the bonfire, looking at the snapshots and names of his campers in the hopes of getting a head start at recognizing his charges. Only time would tell if that had paid off.

But it had kept his mind off Miz Magarry.

She was sure something nice to look at. And for whatever perverse reason, her standoffish attitude had him wondering just what she was like once you broke through her icy shell. Would he get a chance to find out? He had three weeks to try.

Grinning, Jake tucked his schedule in his pocket and headed out.

"Morning." Jake nodded to the lanky young man who was just passing the cabin. "Sean, right? I'm Jake."

"Yeah, that's me. Nice to meet you." He smiled, his teeth a riot of color. "First time here?"

Jake chuckled. "That obvious?"

Red crawled up the boy's neck. "No. It's just that we—my mom and me—come here every year. I don't remember meeting you. We don't always hit every session though. Depends on how much time she can get off work."

"Yeah? What's your mom do?" Which one of the girl's counselors was his mom? Jake didn't think the kid had mentioned a last name. Had he?

"She's a teacher. High school math. She likes the advanced stuff, calculus when she can get it. But mostly she ends up with algebra and geometry."

"A teacher? So doesn't she get summers off?"

Sean shrugged. "Since it's just the two of us, she tries to do summer school when she can. It's not so bad, gives me more time to hang with my grandparents, and they have a pool."

"That's not a bad gig, then. But camp is better?"

"Yeah. More freedom here." Sean winced. "Don't tell my mom I said that. She's great. Just sometimes a little over protective."

"Since I'm not sure which one is your mom, mum's the word."

"Oh. Sorry. I thought everyone knew. Ms. Magarry?"

Jake pursed his lips. Math teacher? He could see that. It fit with his memory of every high school math teacher he'd ever had. Well, everything but those legs. Man. High school teachers hadn't had legs like that when he was a kid. "Just you and your mom?"

"And my grandparents."

What was the story there? Maybe it'd come out in time. "So what's breakfast like here?"

The boy grinned. "You're in for a treat. Cookie always does waffles on the first day. Big fat ones, with all the toppings. Most other days it's eggs, bacon, cold cereal, that kind of thing. It's not so bad. Mom says the eggs are real."

"Awesome." Jake pulled open the screen to the dining hall and held it as Sean and a couple of the female counselors tromped through. The smells eased the clenching of his stomach. Maybe he was hungry, after all.

Sean waited just inside. "Come on, you can sit with us."

Friendly kid. Jake followed the boy through the serving line, heaping his waffle with almost as many toppings as the boy and tossing a couple of slices of bacon on the side of his plate for good measure. He stopped and filled a mug of coffee before angling toward the long table where Deb and Sean were already seated.

"Sean invited me to share your table. That okay?" Jake set his things down without waiting for an answer and tugged out a chair.

The frown disappeared as quickly as it hit Deb's face and she nodded. "Of course. That was nice of you, Sean."

It didn't actually sound as if she thought it was nice, but he'd take it. Any chance to spend extra time unraveling the mystery of Ms. Magarry was welcome. "Thanks. He's a good kid. You must be proud."

"I am." She poked at the pile of fruit salad on her plate and eyed her son's waffle.

Sean followed her gaze and scooted his plate away. "Mom. If you want a waffle, go get one. You're not picking at mine."

She sighed. "I don't *want* a waffle. Just a taste."

"Get your own."

Jake snickered and sliced off a piece of his, dropping it onto her plate. "Here. They're almost the same. And I have no qualms about going back up for seconds."

Deb stared at her plate. "I...you don't need..."

"Dude. You're awesome. Thanks." Sean reached across the table with a raised palm.

Jake gave him five and turned his attention to what was left of his waffle. The kid was right, Cookie knew how to make waffles. Maybe it wasn't rocket science, but to churn out as many as she did without them getting soggy? That took skill. "These are good."

Deb continued to stare at her plate.

Sean nudged his mom with his elbow. "Say thank you."

She was even prettier when she blushed. Jake shook his head. "Don't worry about it, Miz Magarry."

She huffed out a breath. "Thank you. That was generous of you."

"All on the same team, right?" Jake sliced another large chunk of waffle, folded it over, and stuffed it in his mouth.

"You know what you're doing when campers arrive, Sean?"

The boy rolled his eyes. "Yes, Mom. Same thing as last year. I'm on the cabin table. After kids check in with you, they come to me and I point out their counselor. It's not hard."

"I know. Sorry. I worry. What about you, Mr. McGill?"

"I thought we agreed on Jake?" He shrugged. "I know my assigned spot in the lodge. Once everyone's checked in, I take them to the cabin and help them get settled. I think I'll be okay. And Dennis said he'd help out if I got confused."

"Of course he will. He's been coming here for ages."

"Yeah, he's cool." Sean scraped the last bits of topping off his plate and gazed at the serving line.

"Go get another one. I wouldn't want you to starve." Deb smiled as Sean jumped to his feet and took off. She turned to Jake. "Do boys ever stop eating like there's an impending food shortage?"

Jake chuckled. "Maybe when he's thirty. I'm just starting to slow down. A little."

Deb took a small bite of the waffle. "Mm. Those are good. Thanks, again, for sharing. I should probably get to the lodge and make sure everything is set."

"All right." He watched her stalk off, the khaki skort fluttering around her legs. She'd been a little less hostile this morning. Maybe it was stress and she'd calm down once the kids arrived.

JAKE SIGHED and collapsed onto the bed. One day down, only twenty-one to go. He groaned. What had he been thinking? Right. That he'd only have to take kids on hikes and teach them to shoot. This whole cabin counselor thing was way outside his skill set. He listened to the whispers and giggles in the main room. Should he go in there and tell them to stop or give them some leeway? It was the first night, didn't that mean they should get a little extra time?

He sat up and grabbed his phone off the nightstand. He'd give them twenty minutes and then go in and lay down the law if they hadn't settled down. At least no one was crying for home. He wasn't equipped to deal with sniffling little boys who wanted their mom.

Deb, he'd heard all the other counselors call her that, had watched him all day. Everywhere he went, she popped up. There were two new female counselors. She wasn't watching them nearly as much as she was him. He'd started to ask her what the deal was. Twice. Maybe it was just the over-protective single mom thing? He'd wait a little, see if she let up. Not that he'd minded having her around. She was easy to look at. And when she relaxed, as she had a couple of times, she was funny and interesting. He wanted to get to know her better.

Jake grabbed his laptop and fired it up. Thankfully, there was plenty of cell service up here. Kids weren't allowed to have phones, although he'd seen a couple of them being pocketed when they thought he wasn't looking. Still, it allowed him to make a mobile hotspot and hook his laptop up to the Internet long enough to catch up on any urgent email. Not that there was likely to be any, but keeping up with Gabe and Rick was never boring.

There wasn't anything that needed his attention tonight. So he shot off a quick update on the camp, his upgrade to cabin counselor in addition to his other duties, and logged off. That ought to give them a laugh, if nothing else. He checked the time and cocked his head to the side. Quieter. Even a few soft snores, punctuated by the occasional giggle. He switched off the hot spot and set phone and computer aside.

The door separating his room from the tiny cabin entryway creaked as he opened it. He stepped into the main cabin room where five bunk beds lined the walls. Jake cleared his throat. The giggling stopped and two boys on the far side of the room rolled over. He stood there for several seconds before nodding and slipping back to his room. He'd ask about getting something to lube the door tomorrow. No reason to risk waking the campers if he decided to step out on the porch for two seconds to get some air.

He could be reading. Except...it was more interesting to contemplate Miz Magarry. What made her tick? Sean, for starters. It was obvious she was devoted to her son. How old had she been when she had him? Eighteen? Twenty? Jake shook his head. She didn't look like she was in her mid-thirties. She had to be his age, or even a little younger. Which meant...what? Fifteen? She simply didn't strike him as the kind of woman who was sleeping around at that age.

Of course, people could change. He was living proof of that. And at fifteen he hadn't been a saint, though his vice had been drinking. Most of the parties the popular kids had thrown were fuzzy memories of arriving and waking up the next day wishing for death as his head threatened to explode and every muscle in his body ached. He'd sobered up for good in college. Wasn't that a hilarious twist? While most kids were stretching their wings and getting into trouble, Jake had finally had enough. Even in the frat, he'd never been big on the parties and women. He'd hung around to be part of the group, but he'd become the master of nursing a single drink long enough that everyone else was too intoxicated to care. At which point he'd dump out what was left and go back to his room and study. The guys—well, except for Rick and Gabe—had assumed he was naturally smart. Truth was, he'd worked his tail off for his degree.

Half-way through his junior year, he'd found Jesus. And that had changed everything. He'd nearly bailed on the fraternity at that point, but Gabe had convinced him to stay in and had covered for him at the events he'd decided he could no longer participate in. Yep. People could change. And maybe having a kid was enough motivation for that to happen. Or maybe there was more to the story. Would she ever share it with him?

4

Deb set her tray down next to Sean. "Is this seat taken?"

"Nope. Have a seat." He grinned and snagged one of the cookies off her tray. "How's the Camp Director doing?"

She chuckled. He was always able to make her laugh. "Tired. But I think things are finally settling down. How about you?"

He shrugged. "It's all pretty good. Though I could do without the stupid rescue drills. I swear Mr. Langsdon enjoys making everyone freak out by throwing the kid dummy into the pool and blowing his whistle."

"It's procedure. He has to make sure you're all paying attention and staying up on your skills."

"Mom, I know. But seriously, it's a pain." Sean frowned and bit into the cookie. "Still, I'm starting to get a tan, so that's something."

It was Deb's turn to frown. "You're wearing your sunscreen, right? I don't want you getting burned."

"Of course."

She held his gaze until she was convinced he wasn't hedging the truth. "Okay. Skin cancer isn't anything to mess around with. You know Gran..."

"I *know*, okay?" He huffed out a breath. "Did you sit here just to nag me?"

Deb's gaze dropped to her plate. It was hard to let go even the little bit that a teenager required. But she had to start giving him some space. This was the right place to do it, where he was surrounded by people who would protect him from doing anything really stupid. "Of course not. Sorry. Have you had a chance to shoot yet?"

He grinned, nodding vigorously. "Yeah, today finally. Jake is awesome. He had a session where only two campers showed, so he said I could stay as long as I wanted. He hung out through his free time with me. He said he'd teach me to shoot standing, sitting, and kneeling, too if I wanted. Not just the prone position like the campers. And he said I had a good eye that a little extra focus on my breathing would hone. By the time we were done, I was grouping my shots almost close enough that a quarter can cover them. He said to come back anytime, and even if the range was closed, as long as he didn't have something he was supposed to be doing, he'd come and we could do a little extra practice."

"That's great. Do you have your target? I'd like to see it." She squashed the ache in her heart as Sean rhapsodized about the one man she'd hoped he'd never meet. Did Jake have to be so cool? Why couldn't he have been uptight and pushed Sean away, saying the range was just for campers? And to offer his free time? Not that he'd have a lot of that, now that he had campers to manage as well, but he still had enough that if Sean followed through, the two of them were going to be spending a lot of time together in the next three weeks. "Just make sure you aren't keeping Mr. McGill from something he's supposed to do."

"Naw, Mom, he's not like that. Jake's not gonna skip out on

his kids. You should hear him talk about them. He's already totally invested in those pipsqueaks. Makes me kinda sad I'm stuck with Mr. Dennis."

"I thought you liked him?"

"Oh, I do. But he's not really into the kids. You know? He's just here 'cause his daughter likes to come and Mrs. Lisa says this is their family vacation time. I think he'd rather go to the beach." Sean shrugged.

Hmm. "This is our family vacation time..."

"Sure. But I don't really like the beach. Neither do you." He grinned.

She smiled. She loved the beach. But once it was clear that Sean would rather do just about anything than go there, she'd stopped thinking of it as a possibility. Family vacations were supposed to be something everyone enjoyed. "Well, if camp stops being something you like to do, you'll tell me. Right?"

"'Course. Same goes."

She nodded. That was unlikely. She'd do whatever he wanted for as long as she could make it work. But she could always try and make it look like it was her ideal vacation. It was working for camp. So far.

"Hey, Jake. You gonna join us?" Sean waved.

Jake ambled closer to the table. "If your mom doesn't mind?"

"Of course not. Your campers all situated?"

Jake nodded toward the long, full table directly behind them. "They're all hanging out with Dennis' campers. There's no room at the inn. I'll keep an eye on them. I know I hadn't intended to be a counselor, but I do understand the responsibility."

Heat crept across her cheeks. "I didn't mean to imply—"

"Don't worry about it." Jake sat and started digging into the pile of noodles on his plate.

"So. Mr. McGill. What do you do when you're not a camp counselor?"

"I work for a military contractor outside D.C."

Sean's eyes lit. "Really? That's cool. I want to join the Marines when I'm eighteen. Mom says I have to go to college first, but I don't see why I need a degree to protect America."

Deb's stomach sank. What was Jake going to say to that? The last thing she needed was someone supporting Sean in his notions. College was her only hope. If she could get him to school, maybe he'd realize there were more opportunities than serving in the Marine Corps like her father. But Sean, like her, had grown up moving around. And then, once her dad retired, they'd moved to a tiny town not too far from this camp. There weren't a ton of social opportunities for high schoolers in a place where a single high school served the entire county and the graduating class was made up of under two hundred kids. But it was a quiet, steady way of life. She loved it. Sean couldn't wait to get out.

"Hmm. College isn't necessarily a bad idea. And it doesn't mean you can't decide to be a Marine afterward. I've worked with many Marines, and members of other services, who did college first and then joined the military. And then you've got a leg up for when you retire and it's time to get another job. Most military retirement isn't going to support you and your family long-term." Jake scooped another bite into his mouth.

Sean's face fell into a sulk. "I guess. It's just dumb. School is boring."

Jake chuckled. "High school? Yeah, I can see that. Except if I could change one thing about my life, it'd be how I handled high school. Either way, though, college is better."

Deb tilted her head to one side. Had Jake really thought high school was boring? Was that why he'd been such a party hound? "What was wrong with your high school experience?"

Jake's gaze darted to Sean then back to Deb. He cleared his

throat. "I...wasn't what you'd call studious. I scraped by. Honestly, I'm not completely sure how I even managed to get in to college, since I didn't start getting my act together until the end of my sophomore year. And it wasn't an immediate change. I'm not sure how kid-friendly that story is, though I'd be happy to talk to you about it another time. It's sufficient to say I had an experience that showed me what I'd become. And I didn't want to stay that person."

Deb nodded as a lump formed in her throat. She could probably guess what that experience was. It had changed her life, too. She pushed back her chair and grabbed her tray. "I should probably go. There's lots of...coordinating that needs to happen."

SHE MADE it through the rest of the day on autopilot, skipping the evening campfire and locking herself in her room in the lodge instead. There was no way she could handle seeing Jake again. Not after what he said at lunch.

Had he really turned his life around?

He was here, giving up his vacation time, to help at a kid's camp. That said something. And he did military contracting. You couldn't be a drunk and do that, could you? She was past falling for the handsome and charming bad boy. Even if he was, what did that mean to her? Nothing. She had Sean to think about. It didn't—couldn't—matter that her heart skipped a beat every time she saw him.

"Mom?" Sean's voice carried through the door, followed by a knock. "You in there?"

Deb sighed and went to the door. She opened it, unable to stop the smile. He was such a tall young man now. Her baby, yes. But so big now. "Shouldn't you be at the campfire?"

He shook his head. "It's over. You didn't come, I was worried."

"I'm okay. Just needed a few minutes to myself. And I know Gary can handle a campfire without me there. You're probably the only one who noticed I missed it."

Sean smirked as he stepped in and shut the door. "Not quite. Jake was looking for you. He asked about you, oh-so-casually, three or four times. I think he's into you."

Heat washed over her and she struggled to control her face. "Oh?"

"Yeah." He cocked his head to the side. "You know I'm okay with that, right?"

"You're okay with what?"

"You dating. Even getting married, if that's what you want." Sean lifted a shoulder. "That might be cool, actually."

Deb blinked and sat on the edge of her bed. She'd never brought it up with him, though she talked over all the other aspects of their life. She sighed. "I wasn't planning to think about it 'til you were out of the house. There's no rush."

"Seriously? Come on, Mom, you're still young. You've given up a lot for me. I know that. Maybe it's time to think about yourself for once."

She shook her head. She wasn't seriously going to take dating advice from her fifteen-year-old son, was she? "Nah. You're my priority. Always will be."

"Mom." Sean sat next to her. "Dating someone doesn't make me less of a priority. I know that. I'm fifteen now, almost sixteen. I'll be driving soon. I'm already out most weekends with friends anyway. And you're doing what? Sitting at home grading papers. You should have a life, too."

A life? Sean was her life. Had been since she'd convinced her parents she could be responsible and raise him if they would help. And they'd made it clear they were only helping.

He was her responsibility. She didn't regret a second of it. "Well, I'll think about that this fall, then."

"What about Jake?"

"What about him?" Deb crossed her arms.

Sean frowned. "He likes you. It's pretty easy to see that. You could spend some time with him, get to know him. Maybe he'd be someone worth dating."

She shook her head. "He lives near D.C. That's what, five hours? Six?"

"So? It's doable. They probably even have schools up there."

"Whoa. That's quite a leap you're making. From getting to know someone to moving closer? Besides, grandma and grandpa are down here. They're retired and happy with small town life. They aren't going to move up to D.C."

"And we'd only be five or six hours away." Sean smiled. "Just think about it, okay? I like him. He's cool."

Cool. As opposed to the fuddy-duddy she'd become? She squeezed him tightly as he kissed her cheek and eased back out the door. *Jesus? I could really use some guidance here. There has to be a reason Jake's back in my life—but is that reason from You? Help me. Please.*

5

J ake sat out on the porch of the cabin and looked up at the stars. You could see so much more in the night sky out here than at home. It was more like Germany. He missed it. Not just the adventure of the occasional embedding into a deployed team, though that had certainly gotten the adrenaline pumping. Being overseas, in a culture so different from what he grew up in...he'd loved it. And the history. He and Rick had been able to see so much history on their off days. They'd hardly spent any time relaxing in the apartment. Castles. Walled cities. Things you couldn't find in America no matter how hard you searched.

One week of camp was finished. Being a counselor wasn't as bad as he'd expected. Sure, there were the occasional issues between the boys—you couldn't live together constantly and not have squabbles—but so far they'd been easy enough to diffuse. His cell buzzed. Frowning, Jake glanced at the screen. No one had called him all week. But now...

"Hey, Gabe. Everything okay?"

Gabe chuckled. "Yeah. Just checking in. Your email updates

are short and to the point. I wanted to hear your voice, make sure it was really as fun as you said."

Jake shook his head and leaned back on his elbows, clamping the phone to his ear with a shoulder. "It is. It's beautiful down here. The kids are good."

"And the other staff?"

"They're good. Everyone kind of does their thing, you know? We only really see each other at meals and nightly campfires."

"Anyone interesting?"

Jake scoffed. Leave it to the engaged man to expect love to appear behind every cabin door. Deb's face came to mind but he pushed it away. If anyone gave off not interested signals, it was her. "Just about everyone is married or too young. I'm not here for that, anyway."

"Uh-huh. What about the ones who don't fit into the 'just about' classification?"

"You're an idiot."

"Hmm. She sounds lovely. Tell me more."

Jake laughed and scrubbed a hand over his face. "Fine. There's one woman, Deb. She's the camp director. But she barely has two words for me anymore. I thought maybe we were starting to be friends, but since Tuesday she's been distant. Almost like she's avoiding me."

"Ah. A challenge."

He sighed. "I guess. But there doesn't seem to be much point. I'm only here two more weeks. She lives in the valley. With her son."

"Her son? Is that the problem?"

Was it? Jake shook his head. "Nah. He's a good kid. I like him. A lot. In many ways, he makes the package that much more appealing. I don't think she's interested though. And again. They're settled here. Six hours away from where I now live."

"True. And people have never moved from one place to another for love."

Jake laughed. "All right. Fine. But two weeks, man."

"Sounds to me like you'd better get busy."

How would he even go about that? She'd been avoiding him. Granted, he hadn't exactly been seeking her out, but still. Whatever. Better to let it go. "How's everything at IA?"

"IS THIS SEAT TAKEN?" Jake dropped to the grass next to Deb. The lawn, such as it was, in front of the lodge was shaded, empty, and out of the typical path of campers going from one activity to the next. "You're a difficult lady to find."

She frowned as she flipped the folder in her lap closed, keeping one finger in her spot. "Did you need me for something?"

"Not really. I just haven't seen you much this week and, talking to a friend back home last night, realized I missed that. So, since it's a lovely Saturday afternoon and I have an hour break before I have to be back at the shooting range, I thought I'd see if I could figure out where you were hiding."

"I'm not hiding. I'm working." She opened the folder and returned her attention to it. "Thanks for stopping by."

Jake laughed and leaned back. He stretched his legs out in front of him and crossed them at the ankles. She clearly didn't have any idea what it took to make someone go away. Unless the men she was used to dealing with were pushovers. That wasn't a terrible thought. Less competition.

"Why are you still here?" Deb huffed out a breath, her frown edging toward a glare.

"'Cause I have an hour to kill and this is a lovely spot full of good company."

She arched her brows. "Really?"

"Sure. Why not? I've enjoyed every conversation I've had with you so far. And this one isn't looking like it's going to disappoint. I like you, Miz Magarry."

"You don't even know me." She slapped the folder closed again and set it on the stack of folders sitting next to her, their tops weighted with a rock.

He shrugged. "Maybe not well, not yet, but I'm getting a picture. You can learn a lot about someone from their child. And I like yours."

Her smile didn't quite reach her eyes. "Why don't you go spend time with him, then?"

Jake chuckled. She was a spitfire. Her hair might not be deep red, but there was enough in that strawberry blonde to give her the temper. "He's working at the pool. They frown on distracting the lifeguards while kids are swimming."

Deb sighed. "What do you want from me, Jake?"

His smile faltered. Her voice was full of hurt and...resignation? Staying past the knee-jerk brush-off was one thing, but if she really didn't want him around, he wasn't going to force himself on her. Jake stood, brushing off the back of his shorts. "I'd thought maybe we could be friends. I was wrong. Sorry."

Jake tucked his hands in his pockets and strode up the gentle hill toward the path that led out to the rifle range. Maybe he'd shoot a few rounds before the campers arrived. He'd get everything set out and see what kind of time he had.

He waved to Sean as he trudged past the pool. The boy grinned and waved back. Jake sighed. He really liked that kid. But if his mom was set against even being friends, could he still be friends with Sean? He'd never balanced on that particular tightrope before, but it seemed to him that anyone who was an influence in a kid's life should at least be someone the parent respected. Which meant what? He didn't want to hurt Sean. But he also didn't want Deb to think he was using her boy to try and weasel his way into her sphere. There had probably been men in her life who did just that. He wasn't going to be one of them.

6

"What did you do to Jake?" Sean crossed his arms, a sullen pout forming on his lips.

The pressure in her head that had been building since that afternoon exploded. Deb patted the seat next to her in the empty dining hall. "What do you mean?"

Sean dropped into a chair, leaving an empty spot between them. "I went to hang out at the range when I was finished at the pool and he's all, 'Does your mom know you're here?' I mean, what's that about? I thought we were friends."

"Oh, Sean." Deb gave in and rubbed her temples. It didn't do anything for the headache that was rapidly moving into migraine territory. "I didn't...I'll talk to him."

"Just don't. You always do this. Someone shows even the slightest interest in you and before I know what's happening, they're not only no longer interested in you, they're running away from me, too. You say I'm the reason you don't date, that you want me to always be your first priority. But it feels like I'm just an easy excuse. My dad, whoever that was, did a number on you, I get that, but do I have to be the one who constantly pays for it?" Sean stood up, his chair tipping over and clattering to the floor. He opened his mouth as if he had more to say then frowned, his eyes turning flat before he spun on a heel and huffed from the room.

Deb lowered her head to the table and swallowed the burning lump in her throat. Her eyes stung and her head pounded in time with her racing heart. *Why, God? Why did You bring Jake here? Did I do something wrong and this is punishment? I know that's not how You operate, I do...but it feels like it. What am I supposed to do?*

Someone cleared their throat.

Deb shrank inside. Now what? Wiping her eyes on her sleeve, she peeked out. Of course it was Jake. She dropped her head back down. Why wouldn't he just go away?

"So...I was looking for cookies and I kind of overheard the last part of that. I'm sorry. I wasn't trying to hurt Sean. But I also didn't want to overstep. I'm sorry."

She sighed and sat up. "You said that already."

Jake tapped the back of the chair next to her. "Can I sit?"

"Whatever."

He straddled the chair, his arms resting on the back. "Is it okay if Sean spends time with me? He's a good kid and I like having him around."

Her heart twisted. Sean was a good kid. She probably didn't tell him that enough. And he liked shooting. And Jake. "Of course. I'll make sure he knows."

"What about you?"

She frowned. "What do you mean?"

"Any chance you'd spend some time with me?"

Deb blinked. She should say no. Seeking him out—practically stalking him—in high school had led her to making the biggest mistake she'd ever made. Though she couldn't regret Sean. And Jake...still pulled at her. After all these years, one look at him in the camp director's office and her insides had melted into a puddle of goo. But she wasn't a reckless teenager anymore. She was a mother. Which meant she had more to worry about than her own personal desires. "I don't know. I have Sean to think about."

One corner of Jake's mouth twitched up. "He sounded like he'd be okay with it."

Fine. Mentioning Sean wasn't the right first step. Her son wouldn't thank her for it, either. The pounding in her head made it hard to organize her thoughts. "I'm camp director. I can't—there's no time."

"There's meal time. And evenings, after the campers are in bed. You could come sit on the porch and chat, or watch the stars. Both."

Could she? Her heart yearned for the picture that formed in her mind of the two of them under the stars. Before she could stop herself, she nodded. "Okay."

"Swing by tonight?"

Cute wasn't the right word, though the boyish, hopeful grin on his face still made that the first word that popped into her mind. Her head throbbed and a tiny, glowing line began to wiggle through her vision. Aura. Great. Pain stabbed through her left eye. She grimaced. "Can't."

"Are you all right?"

"No. Migraine." Deb clutched her head. Her stomach clenched, acid swirling into nausea. How was she going to get back to her room? The last one she'd had that was this bad had brought vertigo with it.

Jake stood. "Should I go get the nurse?"

"No. I just need to get to bed."

"Okay. Take my arm. I'll walk you."

"You will?"

"Of course." Jake slipped his arm around her waist.

Deb's head dropped to his shoulder and she leaned in, letting her eyes slip closed and willing her feet to move. She'd let Jake take her back to her room, take some medicine, and worry about the rest of it all tomorrow.

SHE HADN'T SEEN Jake all morning in her periodic breaks from the camp director office. Saturdays were much like any other day at camp. He probably had several hikes to lead and a session at the rifle range. Maybe two. But he should be in the dining hall for lunch. Her pulse sped up. Had she really agreed to spend time with him? For all they had a child together, she didn't really know him. High school had been a fierce crush, but they'd never really talked. She wanted to.

When the phone rang she frowned and picked up the handset. So much for getting to lunch early. "Camp director's office, this is Deborah."

"Ms. Magarry? This is Nolan Pershing's mother."

"Hi, Mrs. Pershing, what can I do for you?"

"Well, you see, it's Nolan's first year at camp. And I haven't heard from him so I was concerned that something might be wrong."

Deb fought a grin. "I saw Nolan this morning at breakfast. He's doing well and seemed excited for an extended session at the pool today. Generally the kids are encouraged to send a postcard or letter on Tuesday, so it's very likely your note will arrive today."

"Oh. Hm. But since I called, would it be possible to say hello? Just for a minute?"

"I'm sorry, but no. The office isn't anywhere near the majority of the activities, so I have no convenient way to find him and bring him to the phone. Plus, we discourage kids from doing more than sending a note each week in order to keep homesickness at bay." Deb rubbed the back of her neck.

"Okay. If you see him, will you tell him I called and that I love him? Maybe...maybe remind him to send a note home?"

"Of course, Mrs. Pershing." Deb hung up and shook her head. She couldn't blame the woman. That was one of the reasons she'd always volunteered. Leaving Sean for three weeks wasn't something she was sure she'd be able to handle. He didn't seem to mind. And now that he was older, they didn't spend much time together at camp anyway. But she liked being close.

She stood and brushed at her shorts. Silly. She looked like she always did. And he'd seen her crying and with a migraine. Camp wasn't the place to try and win beauty awards anyway. Deb pulled the door to the office shut and checked that it was locked. She turned and rammed into a broad chest.

"Oof."

Jake chuckled, his hands closing around her arms. "Careful."

"Sorry. I was hoping I'd bump into you."

"And you did."

Heat flooded her face. "I didn't mean..."

"I know. I was teasing. You have time for a lunch break?"

"Yeah. How's your Saturday going?" She turned toward the path that led to the dining hall.

Jake tucked his hands in his pockets and shrugged. "Typical day. Had two hikes this morning. Now I'm free 'til three when I have a riflery session. Sean was thinking he'd swing by around two when he finished at the pool."

This was the first time Sean had latched on to someone so fast. She swallowed against the swift pang that struck her. "Good. He's always loved the rifle range. It was something he was sad to miss when he switched to CIT. I appreciate you letting him shoot."

He grinned. "He's got good aim. Good technique. Whoever taught him did a great job."

"Thanks."

His eyebrows lifted. "You?"

She nodded. "Shooting was something my dad and I always did together. For as long as I can remember."

"Is he a hunter?"

"Nope. Just targets. Cans on the fence. Old computer parts. Whatever he could haul out to someplace deserted enough for us to blow it apart. Drove my mother nuts. She was convinced it wasn't ladylike."

Jake chuckled. "Maybe not in the strict sense of the word, but it's a good skill to have."

"That's what Daddy always told her." Deb grinned. "When Sean came along...Dad finally had the boy he'd always wanted."

"But you taught him to shoot? Not your dad?"

"Dad helped. But since Sean and I come to camp every year, this was a natural place for me to get him more practice."

"Hmm."

She turned and eyed him. "What?"

"You still any good?"

She laughed. "You bet."

"Prove it."

∽

DEB STRETCHED out on the thin foam mat and took the BB gun in her hands. She loaded the BBs, pumped the gun, and settled the stock into her shoulder. She shifted, settling her elbows in a more comfortable place on the mat, and bent her right knee slightly for better stability before angling her head so she could look down the sights toward the target. Deep breath in. Slowly let out half. Squeeze the trigger. Exhale.

She grinned and flipped the gun over to pump more air. She couldn't see the hole in the target, which meant she'd either missed completely or gone through the bulls eye. She was banking on the latter.

When she finished her tenth shot, she set down the gun and sat up. "Well?"

Jake gestured to the target. "Go grab it and we'll see."

Deb laughed and stood, brushing dirt off the front of her shirt. "I see those mats are as clean as ever."

Jake shrugged, holding out his hand for the target as she returned.

"Still got it." Deb poked her finger through the nickel-sized grouping of shots, all in the center of the target.

Jake whistled. "Nice. Why aren't you teaching rifelry?"

"Sometimes I fill in. But I'd rather shoot than show someone what they're doing wrong. I do enough of that in my day job."

"Math teacher, right? You like it?"

"You know what? I really do. There's something about helping a kid see that math can be beautiful, not scary. That's its own reward." She didn't need to mention the rarity of that success. Most days were full of trying to convince her students that it didn't matter whether or not they thought they'd use it in real life, the State of Virginia required them to learn it if they wanted to get on with that process. "Do you enjoy your job?"

"I do. It's been a bit of a change this year, though. Until February, I was living in Germany. Rick, he's another of the three founders of the company, and I handled liaising with onsite military personnel. Sometimes that meant we stayed on base, other times we shipped out with them for a while. It was...something special. But things changed and now we're back home." Jake shrugged. "It's taken some getting used to."

She could imagine. Living overseas though...that was a secret dream. One she'd had since before high school. "Would you go back? If you could?"

"In a heartbeat. Gabe, he's the third founder, is in the beginning stages of some negotiations that might end up with someone needing to go to Italy. I plan to be that someone if it happens."

"Where in Italy?"

"Not sure yet, to be honest. And it may not happen. But I've pretty much decided that I'm going back to Europe at some point next year. Even if it's just vacation."

Deb sighed. "That's one of my dreams. I make do with summer camp. But one of these days, I'm going to get across the ocean. I'd love to take Sean for his high school graduation, but..."

"Hey, Mom. What are you doing out here?" Sean, still wearing his swim trunks with a white t-shirt and a towel draped around his neck stopped at the entrance to the pergola that kept sun and rain off campers while they shot.

"Thought I'd come and show Jake how it's done." Deb offered her target to her son, grinning as his eyes widened.

"Nice." He looked at Jake. "Still okay if I shoot?"

"Of course. You wanna try kneeling today?" Jake took another gun down from the storage rack and offered it Sean.

"Nuh-uh. Sitting is weird enough. Let me stick with that a little longer."

"All right. Go get set up." Jake glanced at Deb. "You want to go again?"

Something in his eyes warmed her. It was heady. Potent. "I don't think so. Can I stay and watch?"

Jake grinned. He dragged a stool out of the shed where all the supplies were stored and dusted off the top. "I'd like nothing better."

7

Jake checked the time and set his laptop aside. What was that? The sounds at night were usually animal in nature —owls, crickets, that sort of thing. But that had a distinctly human ring to it. He waited, listening. Just as he was about to return to his email, it happened again. Puffing out his cheeks, Jake stood and tiptoed out of his room to stand in the doorway of the boys' big sleeping room.

"Uhhhhhh." One of the boys, Andrew, moaned from the bottom bunk across the room.

Jake went to the boy's side and squatted down, his voice low. "Hey, man. What's wrong?"

"It hurts."

Jake frowned and laid his hand on Andrew's forehead. It was hot. "Where?"

"My stomach."

"You need the nurse. Hang on a second." Jake patted the boy's leg and hurried out of the room, skipping down the steps to his cabin. He jogged up the path to the next cabin and tapped on the screen.

Dennis shuffled out, his eyes heavily lidded. "What's up, man?"

"I've got a sick camper...were you asleep?"

Dennis nodded. "Yeah, about this time it always starts catching up with me, so I go to bed at lights out. What do you need?"

"Can Sean come hang out in my cabin while I run the kid down to the nurse?"

"'Course. I'll send him right down."

Jake nodded. "Thanks. I'd better get back."

He hurried back to the cabin. Andrew's moans reached the porch. Jake winced. Poor kid. He clearly felt terrible. *Dear Jesus, please help Andrew feel better. Help me know what to do.*

"Hey there. Still hurting?"

The boy nodded, his eyes unfocused.

"Can you walk?"

Andrew tried to sit up but fell back on his pillow with a loud groan.

"I'll take that as a no. All right, I'm going to carry you. Put your arms around my neck, okay?"

"'K."

Jake shoved back the covers and scooped the boy into his arms. Heat pumped off Andrew's body. As he stood, he spotted Sean in the doorway. "Thanks, Sean. You can hang out in my room if you want, or here. I don't know how long this'll be though, so make yourself at home."

"I got this, no worries. Is that Andrew?"

Jake nodded.

"Aw. Hang in there, man. We need you at the pool tomorrow."

The boy tried to smile but ended up groaning.

"Thanks again, man."

Sean nodded and made a shooing motion.

Jake grinned and took off down the path, trying not to jostle

Andrew but still wanting to get to the nurse quickly. Between the sliver of moon and the solar lights on the path, the trip was almost as easy in at night as it was during the day. He still had one near tumble when he turned from the cabin path to the main loop that headed down to the lodge and the nurse's quarters. He took the stairs to the lodge two at a time, scooted through the recreation area, and knocked at the nurse's door. He counted to ten in his head before knocking again.

Still belting her robe, the nurse opened her door with a frown. "Yes?"

"I know it's late, sorry. But Andrew here isn't feeling well."

The nurse reached out and laid her hand on the boy's forehead. Her eyebrows lifted. "Bring him in. Any other symptoms?"

"He said his stomach hurts."

Andrew moaned.

"Hi there, Andrew. Can you show me where it hurts?"

The boy rubbed abdomen.

The nurse frowned. "Can you stand up for me please?"

Jake set Andrew down and steadied him as he got his balance.

"Do you think you can jump up and down?"

Andrew shook his head.

"Try? For me?" The nurse smiled.

Andrew gave a little hop and collapsed on the floor sobbing.

Jake cleared his throat. "Shouldn't we give him something?"

The nurse shook her head as she picked up the phone and dialed. "I'm calling Ms. Magarry. He needs to go to the emergency room. Based on where he showed me he hurt and that reaction I think he might have appendicitis. I wouldn't be comfortable ignoring those—"

She stopped talking to Jake and explained the situation to Deb. "She's on her way over."

There was a rapid knock at the door.

"That was fast." Jake moved out of the way as the nurse bustled to the door and pulled it open.

Two girls, along with a female counselor, stood outside the door. "Hi, sorry. The girls aren't—"

One of the girls vomited at the nurse's feet. The other began to sob. Jake reached for the trash can beside the nurse's desk and handed it to the vomiting girl while the nurse ushered them into the room.

"Go lie down on the bed in the corner. Take the can with you." She pressed her hand to the sobbing girl's forehead and sighed. "You go lie down in the bed next to her."

Jake scanned the room. "Is there a mop or some paper towels? I can take care of that."

"That would be fabulous. In the closet over there." The nurse tossed him a grateful smile and unlocked a cabinet that hung on the wall.

In the closet, Jake found a roll of paper towels, a bucket, and a sponge. He stopped at the infirmary sink and ran some water into the bucket before squatting down to scoop as much of the vomit into paper towels as he could. That done, he dunked the sponge into the water and swiped at the floor.

"I'm pretty sure cleaning floors wasn't one of the jobs I mentioned when I made you a counselor." Deb smiled as she stepped into the room and looked around. "Nurse Jane, you called?"

The nurse looked up from where she perched on the edge of the bed next to one of the girls and nodded toward Andrew, who still lay curled in a ball on the floor. "He needs the ER. I was going to say I'd go with you, but now..."

"I can go by myself. That's fine." Deb stepped around the clean but wet spot on the floor and knelt by Andrew. "Come on, let's get you to the hospital. Can you walk?"

Andrew shook his head, tears leaking out of his eyes.

Jake dropped the sponge into the bucket and stood. "I'll carry him to your car."

"I need his medical release forms before we leave." Deb looked over at the nurse. "If you just tell me where you store them?"

The nurse pointed to the desk.

Jake washed his hands at the sink. "It's Andrew Harris."

"Thanks." Deb rooted through the file drawers and drew out a manila folder. She flipped through it quickly. "Ready?"

"Sure." Jake scooped up Andrew. "Lead on."

"Let me grab my cell. I'll call his mom on the way." She frowned, tapping the folder against her leg. "Maybe you should come. If I can't carry him from here to the car, how am I going to get him into the hospital?"

They probably had a wheel chair, or a gurney or something. On the other hand, this would be some time alone with Deb. Something that was in short supply under normal circumstances. Jake grinned. "Sure thing. Sean's hanging in my cabin with the boys."

"That's fine, then. I'll text Dennis and let him know, that way if we're not back before breakfast, he'll pitch in. Come on."

Jake followed behind her. It wasn't quite ten p.m. Was it possible they wouldn't be back by breakfast? His heart skipped a beat. That was a lot of time alone with Deb. Granted, there'd be a sick kid in the room. But still. What was it his mom used to say? Make hay while the sun shines.

"I FOUND a little coffee shop that was still open, got you a latte." Jake held out the tall, insulated cup as he sat next to her. The hard, plastic chairs in the waiting area were a surprise. Most emergency rooms he'd been to at least tried to make the waiting process pleasant. "Any luck getting a hold of Andrew's mom?"

Deb shook her head. "The form says that she and her husband go on vacation while the kids are at camp, so I don't know what that means. I was positive parents were required to give a contact number that could be reached at any time. And that they were supposed to be able to get to the camp within a few hours if something went wrong. Maybe I just assumed all parents are like me."

Jake shook his head. "Nope. If all parents were like you, I wouldn't have been able to grab a spot helping out. They'd all have been full. You're dedicated. And your son is proof that you've been that way his entire life. He's a great kid."

"He is."

A nurse strode over before Deb could continue. "They've got Andrew back from ultrasound and he's being prepped for surgery. Everything should be fine. There are more comfortable chairs in the surgical waiting room if you want to head that way. You can follow the signs."

"Surgery? That's fast." Jake stood and looked at Deb. "I didn't think they'd move that fast."

"While you were hunting up coffee, they got the test results back. His appendix hasn't ruptured, but it's imminent. They want to get in there before that. Thankfully our forms give us the ability to authorize whatever we need to, so it's not critical that we get a hold of his parents. Except that if it was me, I'd want to be here. You know?"

He nodded and studied the sign above them, gesturing to the left corridor. "I do. We'll keep trying to call. Did they say how long the surgery would be?"

"About an hour for the surgery. But there's prep and recovery and then he'll have to stay...I think they said at least twenty-four hours?" Deb frowned. "We're going to have to work something out with the staff at camp if we can't get in touch with his mom. I don't want to leave him here alone."

"We'll keep calling. Oh hey, here we are. These chairs do look more comfortable. How about over here where we can stretch out a little?"

Deb followed his pointing finger and nodded. "Sure. I'm going to try calling again. Then...maybe you can tell me that long story you mentioned the other day?"

Jake swallowed. He'd been half-hoping she'd forget about that. It wasn't a secret. He told everyone he was interested in—it was a matter of honesty. Full disclosure. So it wasn't as if he would've been able to put it off indefinitely. While Deb punched in Andrew's mom's phone number, he wandered over to the bank of seats he'd pointed out and sat. He dug his own cell out of his pocket and texted Gabe with a request to pray for Andrew. And that they'd be able to get a hold of his mom. When he was done, he said a quick prayer himself.

His nerve endings jangled. Telling someone about his past had never caused this much anxiety. What, if anything, did that mean? Maybe it just meant he was thinking too hard. Or that he enjoyed Sean's company. And if Deb decided Jake shouldn't be around her kid...he'd respect her wishes. But it would break his heart.

"Finally got her." Deb collapsed into the seat next to Jake and tucked her phone into her purse. "They're in Puerto Rico. So she's going to see if she can move their flight and get out as soon as possible."

"Yikes. They left the country?"

"That was my question. According to her, she didn't see why it would be a problem, seeing as how Puerto Rico is a United States territory. Maybe we need to make it clear they need to be within a certain number of hours distance. That's a problem for another day." Deb smiled, her eyes weary. "So, high school?"

Jake rubbed the back of his neck as heat crawled up it. "I had a drinking problem—a big one—the first two years of high school. If there was a party, I was at it and probably drunk within the first five minutes. It got to the point that, in order to get the fastest buzz, when I knew there was a party, I wouldn't eat all day so the alcohol would hit faster. Half-way through the ninth grade, I started having blackouts."

Deb nodded.

"Half-way through sophomore year, I realized I needed to straighten up."

"Just like that?"

Jake cleared his throat. "Not exactly. It never bothered me because I figured I wasn't hurting anyone but myself. My friends said I was just a lot of fun. Until one night I ended up hurting someone. Only I didn't find out about it for two weeks. By then it was too late to even try to make right."

"What happened?"

"From what I was told—and I only know what my friends said—I...slept with someone. I don't know her name. They weren't sure who she was. Everyone said she was into it, chasing me, even. But that doesn't matter. That I could do something like that and not know it?" Jake squeezed his eyes shut. Would he ever be clean of that stain? Jesus had forgiven him. But how was he supposed to forgive himself when he couldn't apologize? Couldn't try to make things right? "I knew it had to stop."

"Did it?"

Jake nodded. "Yeah. I slipped up once more that year when I thought I could go to a party and not drink. But no one was having that. I'd been the funniest guy around, I guess, and they weren't ready for me to give it up. So I caved to the peer pressure. The next day I promised myself I wouldn't go to another party in high school. And I didn't."

She nodded.

"What about you? You know my biggest failure. Did you do anything stupid in high school that has you cringing still today?"

8

"Well, I'm thirty and my son just turned fifteen. So...there's that."

Jake winced. "Sorry. I don't always think before I speak."

Deb laughed. The red staining his neck and cheeks was kind of endearing. But it didn't stop the muscles clenching in her belly. She'd tried to play it off, but if he pushed...what was she supposed to say? "Other than that? Not really."

Jake nodded. "Sean's dad? Is it okay to ask?"

Her heart stopped then resumed beating in double time. "He's...not in the picture."

"I'm sorry. I don't get someone who could walk away like that. That must have made it even harder."

She swallowed. She should leave it like that. Just let him assume the worst. It wasn't as if that never happened. But...Deb sighed. "It's not quite like that. I never told him I was pregnant. He doesn't know about Sean."

Jake's eyebrows rose. "Oh."

He must think she was a horrible person. Words of explanation scrambled up her throat, clamoring to get out. But did she really owe him that? He had no reason to suspect anything. Still. "My family moved out of the area before I knew. By the time I realized...there didn't seem to be any point. Besides, it's not as if we'd been dating long-term. It was kind of a one-time thing. I'm not proud of it. I knew what I was doing though. As it is, I can't wish it away—wouldn't even if I could. Sean is...everything to me."

"I can see that. From what I've observed, you're a good mom." Jake offered a thin smile.

Her heart sank. What wasn't he saying? Most likely something about how Sean's father deserved to know, either way. How he ought to be paying child support and have a chance to be involved. It was the same lecture her parents still gave her periodically. Sure, they supported her decision to parent—or they'd come around, at least—but they wanted to see her married, for Sean to have a dad. Deb wanted those things too. But not with someone who was roped into it because of one night. Especially now that she knew Jake had no recollection of the event. How would that be fair?

And yet...getting to know Jake now? He'd not only be a great dad, he was someone she could see in her life. It wasn't the same infatuation she'd had in high school, but the stirring when he was near, the hope that their hands might brush, that was all familiar. Throw in the fact that he appeared to have grown into a solid man of God? She sighed. "Thanks. I try."

"Do you ever take time for you?"

"Sure. Of course I do." Deb frowned.

"So you're seeing someone?"

She laughed. Her mirth trailing off as she studied his expression. "Oh. You're serious? No. I'm not dating. That can wait until Sean's off to college. He's my priority."

"Ah." Jake shifted in his seat, his hands clasping together.

"What does that mean?"

He shrugged. "I was going to ask if you wanted to sit

together at the campfire some night, maybe go for a walk after the campers are bunked down. I've watched Dennis' cabin a few times, well, Sean and I have, while he and his wife have gone for a stroll. Figured he'd probably loan me Sean and keep an eye out if you wanted to do the same."

Breath clogged in her lungs. He was asking her out? Or as much as that was possible while working at a summer camp for kids. She clenched her purse to stop her hands from trembling. "I...think I'd like that."

Jake grinned, reaching over to take her hand. A shiver worked its way up her arm to her spine. She wove her fingers through his.

"So. Other than being a math teacher, camp director, and amazing mom, what else do I need to know about Deb Magarry?"

"OH, ANDREW." A woman stopped in the doorway of the hospital room, her hand flying to her chest. She stepped into the room and moved toward the bed.

Deb stood, rubbing her eyes. She spared a quick glance at Jake who had fallen asleep propped precariously on what the hospital laughably called a bench along the wall. He'd been holding her hand. "Mrs. Harris?"

"Yes. I'm sorry. You're Ms. Magarry?"

"I am. I—could I see some ID?" Deb edged toward the bed where Andrew was resting peacefully.

"Of course." Mrs. Harris smiled and dug into the oversized purse that hung from her shoulder. "My husband is parking the car, he dropped me off at the entrance. I'm glad I grabbed this on my way. Here."

Deb took the driver's license, studied it and Mrs. Harris, and handed it back. "Thanks. I just wanted—"

"Please. I appreciate it. I wouldn't want it any other way. How is he?"

"He's doing well. They removed his appendix before it burst, so it wasn't as bad as it could have been. The nurses said he did well in recovery. They didn't let us up until he was in the room. So we've only been here," Deb peeked at her watch, "two hours? You made good time."

"God had to have been looking out for us. We got the airport as they were starting to board a flight. There was space and they didn't give us any hassle about our tickets once we explained. I think my husband broke records getting here from Richmond after we landed." Mrs. Harris smiled, exhaustion evident in her expression. "I'm so sorry we weren't closer."

Deb nodded. "Let me go find the nurse and explain that you're here now. Then Jake—that's his cabin counselor—and I can get back to camp. Maybe we'll even make it before breakfast."

Mrs. Harris grabbed Deb's arm. "Thank you for taking care of my boy."

Deb smiled, unsure of what to say. It was her job. She would've done the same for anyone. But that probably wasn't the right thing to tell his mother. She slipped past Mrs. Harris and made her way to the nurse's station to explain the situation. Finished, she went back to Andrew's room, pausing in the doorway. Mrs. Harris had dragged a chair beside the bed and was holding her son's hand, her head resting on the mattress. The boy continued to sleep. "Everything's set. So Jake and I will head out. Once they discharge Andrew you can come collect his things at the camp office. I'll make sure they're all packed up and ready for you."

Mrs. Harris glanced up. "Okay. Of course. Thank you again."

Deb crossed the room and gently shook Jake's shoulder. He

was adorable when he slept. It was almost a shame to wake him. "You ready?"

Blinking, Jake sat up. He wiped his mouth and nodded. "Yeah. Sorry. I guess I was more tired than I thought. They're here already?"

She nodded toward Mrs. Harris. "Yep. We should get back in time for breakfast. I think it's pancakes today."

"Pancakes. That might keep me awake until my afternoon break. Then I'm taking a nap."

Deb chuckled. "I suspect that's going to be on my list, too. We'll see you soon, Mrs. Harris."

With another round of thanks and handshakes after Mr. Harris made it to the room, Jake and Deb headed to the elevator. He slipped his hand into hers and tingles spread up her arm. She leaned against him as they went down to the main floor.

Out in the parking lot, Jake pulled open the passenger door and held it for her.

"You sure you're okay to drive?"

He nodded. "The nap I caught was enough. And maybe we'll see someplace we can grab coffee. I don't understand why the cafe closed at midnight. Don't they have people who need coffee all night in a hospital?"

Deb chuckled and slid into her seat. "You'd think, wouldn't you?"

Jake closed her door and headed around the hood of the car. Deb leaned over and unlocked his door. He grinned as he sat.

"What?"

"My mom always told me a girl who unlocked your door for you was a keeper." Jake started the car and reached for his seatbelt. "It's a little harder these days, I guess, with all the automatic locks though. Guess sometimes it pays to have an older vehicle."

She chuckled even as wisps of heat brushed across her cheeks. Was she a keeper? Despite having a son, she had very little actual dating experience. The few times she'd given in and gone out with someone hadn't gone well. Maybe she'd talked about Sean too much? Who knew? The end result was the same. No one had asked her out a second time. But Jake knew Sean—liked him, even. Would that make a difference?

They made minimal conversation on the drive back to camp. Enough to keep Jake awake—though he didn't act as though he was struggling. The coffee they'd stopped for on the way back to the highway had energized her enough to have her thoughts spinning, but not enough for them to make sense. Was she seriously considering a relationship with Jake? Considering? Hadn't she already agreed to it?

Deb sighed and looked out the window as Jake turned onto the road that would lead up to camp. Almost an hour until breakfast. Campers were probably starting to wake and jostle for the showers. Well, the girls were. Some of the boys...she was pretty sure the only bathing the boys were doing involved the swimming pool. At least they kept the chlorine balanced.

Jake pulled his car back into the spot he'd vacated the evening before. "Well."

She let out a breath that was half-way between a laugh and a sigh. "Feels like an eternity ago, but it was only ten hours. Ready for another day?"

"Let's hope so." Jake hopped out of the car and started around to her side.

Deb pushed open her door and climbed out. It was nice that he tried, but she was capable of opening her own doors. And she wasn't going to stand on ceremony. The intention was enough for her. "Thanks, Jake."

"For what?"

"Going with me. Staying. Making the whole ordeal considerably more pleasant than it could have been."

Jake moved closer.

Deb stepped back, bumping against the car.

He put one hand on the car and leaned toward her, his gaze holding hers.

Her heart hammered in her chest. "What are you..."

Jake's lips against hers stopped her objection. Ended her ability to think for a moment, even. Electricity coursed through her body and the yearnings she'd buried the moment she'd laid her eyes on Sean for the first time exploded through her. She met his kiss, her hands sliding up his arms to join behind his neck, pulling him closer. Time stopped.

Gradually, her senses returned as Jake eased back, a smile hovering on his lips. "Well then."

Deb took in a shuddering breath and let it out slowly. "Right. Um. Breakfast?"

Jake grinned. "I'm going to grab a shower, and corral my campers, but then? Absolutely."

She nodded and started toward the lodge.

He grabbed her arm and pulled her back for another toe curling kiss. "To tide me over."

Jake strode toward the cabins, hands in his pockets, whistling.

Deb leaned against his car. She'd just wait here until her legs worked again.

9

Sean had the campers already lined up and ready to head to breakfast when Jake neared the cabin. He smiled. The kid was good. Jake hadn't had them down to the meal precisely on time yet.

"Hey, you're back." Sean grinned. "How's Andrew?"

Jake dragged a hand through his hair. "He's better, now. They had to remove his appendix. So it's good we got him to the hospital when we did. Everything go okay?"

"Sure. They slept. I slept." Sean shrugged. "No big deal. You want to take them to breakfast?"

"Do you mind hanging with them another maybe twenty minutes? I could use a shower. It's been a long night."

"'Course. You okay? I can probably handle whatever you have first if you need a nap. I'd have to clear it with Mr. Langsdon at the pool, but we have plenty of guards."

It was tempting. But Deb was going to be at breakfast. Coffee with her trumped every other tantalizing prospect. Jake shook his head. "I'll meet you down there."

"All right. Let's go, guys." Sean jerked his head toward the path that would take them to breakfast.

Jake climbed the stairs to the cabin then stopped. He turned. "Sean?"

The boy jogged down the line of campers. "Yeah?"

"I asked your mom out. Like a date—well, as much of a date as is possible with everything going on around here."

Sean grinned. "Awesome. She said yes, right?"

Jake nodded. "You're okay with it?"

"Yeah. You're cool. I'm a little surprised you got her to do it though."

Jake chuckled. "Me too, man. I'll be down soon as I can."

Sean waved as he ran to catch up with the campers. Jake smiled as the group started in on their cabin marching song. He hadn't planned to say anything to Sean. But it had seemed right. A boy—young man—needed to know when someone was interested in his mom, didn't he?

JAKE SCANNED THE DINING HALL, fatigue dragging at every muscle. The shower had helped. For about ten minutes. Dressing and getting down here had depleted whatever boost of energy he'd gotten from the hot water and the anticipation of seeing Deb again. Where was she? He frowned and made his way toward the serving line. She wasn't in her usual spot. She hadn't sat with his cabin, though Sean was there. He dropped a scoop of eggs onto his plate. She wasn't here.

He went through the rest of the line on autopilot. He'd need food—and caffeine—to make it through the day, regardless of the lead ball that had settled in his stomach. Had she changed her mind?

"Mom's not here." Sean shook his head as Jake pulled out the chair next to him. "She probably got freaked out and is hiding in her room."

Jake stabbed a bit of eggs. "I was just thinking that. Oh well."

"Aw, man. Don't give up that easy. She's been on like two dates since I was born. And from the pieces she's told me, my biological dad didn't even know who she was when she threw herself at him."

"Hey. I'm not sure you should talk about your mom like that." Jake drew in a deep breath to steady his thundering heart. He clenched his hands into fists. It was just so...disrespectful.

Sean grinned. "See? She needs you in her life. Grandma and Grandpa try, but when I mouth off, they usually let it slide 'cause it's true."

Jake ground his teeth together. "Just because something is true doesn't make it okay to say."

Sean's shoulder jerked in a shrug. "'K. My point, though, is that she goes on and on about how I'm her only priority and that kind of thing. But that's not right. She needs someone to help her see that she matters, too. I'm either joining the Corps or going to college in a few years and I'd rather she not be stuck at home bingeing on TV shows and crying 'cause she misses me when that happens."

Jake couldn't stop the laugh that bubbled up. "I can't picture your mom being that big a mess when you leave, but I see what you're saying. So what do I do?"

Sean drummed his fingers on the table. "Give her a little space for now. She'll come around."

Was he really going to take dating advice from a fifteen year old? On the one hand, the boy probably knew Deb best. On the other...a little space? "I've got a hike starting in ten minutes anyway."

"That's the spirit." Sean stood and grabbed his tray. "Gotta run."

Jake scraped the cold eggs on his plate onto a piece of buttered toast, folded it in half, and took a bite. It wasn't going to win any culinary awards, but it'd silence the growling of his stomach. And maybe Deb would show up for lunch.

Jake checked that the rifle wasn't loaded and hung it back on the rack in the shed. He walked over to the range and scoured the ground for BBs and anything else that shouldn't get left out. There was an hour before dinner and his bed was calling his name. He'd stretch out for a few minutes, maybe surf the web on his phone to keep from falling completely asleep, and then meet up with his campers outside the entrance to the dining hall. The prospect of the evening ahead had him sighing. Dinner, ultimate Frisbee against Dennis' cabin, the evening campfire, and then cabin devotions all had to happen before blissful sleep could be his. And somewhere in there maybe he'd get to see Deb.

She hadn't been at lunch, either. It had taken every last ounce of will power not to stop by her office on the way to his afternoon activities and ask what was going on. Space. He was going to give her some space.

Jake dropped a handful of BBs in the storage container and closed the door to the shed before clicking the padlock into place. Good enough. Shoulders drooping, he turned.

"Hi." Deb leaned against one of the awning's poles, her hands tucked in her pockets.

He blinked, his pulse racing. "Hi yourself."

"Sorry I missed breakfast. And lunch. It's been a crazy day." Deb's head tilted to the side. "How are you holding up?"

He shrugged. "Okay, I guess."

Her tongue darted between her lips. "Apparently when you have to take a camper to the Emergency Room, once you get back there are reams of paperwork that have to be filled out.

And phone calls with insurance people who want to be sure that it wasn't caused by negligence."

"I've never heard of negligence causing appendicitis."

"It was a new one for me, too. I believe the exact quote was along the lines of, 'These are our policies. We can't break them for every situation that doesn't fit perfectly.'"

He snickered. Maybe she'd had good reasons for missing those meals after all. "You win. I just had to hike while exhausted. And of course I ended up with that kid—oh what's her name? The one who'll put anything in her mouth on a dare?"

"Ugh. Jocelyn. What'd she eat this time?"

"I caught her before she put the poison ivy in her mouth, but I'm hoping she's not crazily allergic. That one might end up being considered neglect."

Deb pinched the bridge of her nose. "Identifying poison ivy is part of the pre-hike brief, right? With pictures?"

Jake nodded. "I even point it out for the first ten-ish minutes of the hike. There's no reason anyone wouldn't recognize it."

"Then it's probably fine. I'll check in with the nurse after dinner just in case though." She pushed off the post and took a tentative step toward him. "I really am sorry about breakfast."

He held out a hand, grinning when she took it. He laced his fingers through hers and tugged her closer. "I forgive you. Sean said you were probably getting cold feet. Though I think he used the words 'freaking out'."

"Sean? Why would Sean have a comment one way or the other?"

Jake frowned. Her eyes were wide and she'd gone stiff. "I might have mentioned that I'd asked you out. He seemed pretty excited about the prospect."

Deb closed her eyes and drew in a deep breath. "I'd planned to talk to him...later. I wish you hadn't said anything. Maybe I should go find him and explain."

"Why? What's there to explain?"

She yanked her hand out of his. "I don't date. I—he—has to wonder why I said I'd date you. He probably has questions..."

"Deb." Undeterred, Jake reached for her hand again and squeezed. "Hey, he just wants you to be happy."

She sighed. "I am happy."

"Okay. He wants you to be happier. He's a smart kid, with a good head on his shoulders."

"You're just saying that because he agrees with what you want."

Was he? Maybe. But that didn't meant it was wrong. "It's not what you want?"

"I didn't say that."

"So this is what you want?" His lips curved.

Her smile was coy. "I didn't say that either."

"Well, what do you want?"

Her stomach rumbled. "Right now? Dinner. And someone pleasant and handsome to eat it with."

Jake bit back a sigh. She was good—too good—at deflecting his attempts at a serious conversation. But he'd play along. For now. "As it happens, I can probably help you with that." He offered his elbow. "Shall we?"

10

What was she doing? The last five days—had it really only been five days?—had been like a dream. The same dream her high school self had had, only so much better. She could fall for Jake so easily. But what sort of future was possible between them? To have any sort of chance at a lasting relationship, she'd have to lay it all on the line. Not just telling him about Sean, which was bad enough, but explaining why she'd done it in the first place. How was she supposed to do that when she wasn't sure she completely understood herself? Besides, he'd be leaving at the end of the week.

She and Sean were scheduled through the entire month of July. There was one more three-week camp session booked, with an option for an additional shorter camp if there was enough enrollment. That didn't look likely at this point, but who knew how things would change in the two weeks before the camp made an official decision one way or the other? And even without camp interfering, she and Sean lived down here, in the southern tail of the state. Jake lived up near D.C. She wasn't looking to go back there. Her parents had retired here.

She had a job she...well, she didn't always love it. But she didn't hate it, and that was worth something. She'd made a nice life for herself and for Sean. They were happy. Weren't they?

Deb sighed and pushed back from the desk. She was caught up on the paperwork, finally. And who knew how much of that was required even after camp started? She'd taken the job thinking it was a well-oiled machine as soon as everything started up. In some ways it was. In others? She shook her head. It was almost as bad as teaching.

"Hey, Mom. Got a minute?"

She smiled up at Sean. "Always. What's up?"

Sean dropped into the chair in front of her desk. "Jake wondered if I could help with the fireworks tonight. He said I should ask you."

Deb pursed her lips. "He did, did he? I'm not sure."

"Mom. Come on, please?"

What was it with boys and blowing things up? "Fireworks are dangerous. That's why we needed a counselor who was qualified to set them off in the first place."

Sean crossed his arms, the beginning of a scowl forming.

Deb pinched the bridge of her nose. "What would you be doing?"

"Really?" Sean scooted up in the seat.

"I'm not saying yes. I'm gathering information."

"Just helping set them up, maybe lay the fuses. Nothing dangerous."

She sighed. "I'll talk to Jake."

"Sweet." Sean jumped to his feet. "You're the best, Mom."

"I'm not promising anything."

Sean simply grinned before hurrying out of her office. Deb glanced at the time. Almost time for supper. She'd head over to the dining hall and catch Jake when he arrived. She double-checked that all the important paperwork was in her locked desk drawer, shut down her laptop, and stood.

Outside, she blinked, adjusting her eyes to the daylight. She'd been in the office entirely too much today. With Andrew and his parents coming by for his things and all the out processing paperwork, plus making sure everything was in order for the fireworks tonight there hadn't been time for her usual walks around the camp...or a rendezvous with Jake.

"Going my way?" Jake sauntered around the corner of the building and grinned.

Her heart skipped a beat. How was it possible for him to take her breath away so easily? "I was looking for you, actually."

"Yeah?" A slow grin spread across his face. "Now that you found me, what are you going to do with me?"

She chuckled. "Talk to you about Sean helping with the fireworks."

"Oh." Jake stuck his hands in his pockets. "Is that a problem? I should've asked you before mentioning it, shouldn't I?"

"Well, yeah. You wouldn't let him do any of the lighting? Nothing dangerous?" She sounded neurotic and overprotective, didn't she? It didn't matter if he was fifteen. He was her baby. She was allowed to worry.

Jake shook his head. "Nah. Just helping me make sure each bank is ready for ignition. It's perfectly safe."

Deb let out a breath. He had to grow up sometime. Might as well start trying to let go. "All right."

"Cool. He'll have fun. You want to hang out with us, keep an eye out?" He reached for her hand, twining his fingers through hers.

Would the jolt of contact go away over time? Hopefully not. "No. I trust you. And Sean. Plus, I have to be closer to the rest of the campers in case there's an issue. You're going to be on the other side of the lake, right?"

"Yeah. You'll get a better viewing angle that way. I think you're going to like the show. Once I found out I had complete control over what to bring, I might have gone a little overboard.

But it'll be fun." Jake glanced around before tugging her closer and lowering his mouth to hers.

Sparks shot down her spine to her toes. How did he still have this effect on her? She eased back. "Dinner?"

"Sure. I could eat." Jake started toward the dining hall, his fingers still twined with hers. "Busy day? I looked for you a few times, but didn't see you on any of your usual rounds."

She smiled. He'd missed her.

"MOM. CAN I BORROW YOUR SWEATSHIRT?" Sean pulled open the door to the small closet in her room and started pushing hangers aside. "The grey one with a hood?"

"Sean?" Deb poked her head out from the bathroom. "What do you need?"

"My sweatshirt got wet at the pool. It's getting cool already. On the other side of the lake there's going to be a breeze. I thought I could borrow your hoodie. That okay?"

"I guess. Yeah. Be safe and have fun."

Sean waggled the jacket as he disappeared. Well, at least he'd acknowledged her. And he didn't mind borrowing her sweatshirts. It was probably good she never bothered with the women's cut on things. If it was getting cool, she should grab an extra layer for herself, just in case.

Deb sorted through the hangers and tugged the windbreaker out. Which one had he...her stomach sank. She flipped through the clothes again. Why had she even brought it? That was easy. It was her favorite. Old, broken in, and comfortable, it was perfect for snuggling in during the evening. It was like having a piece of home with her. Sean had borrowed it before...but she had no idea he would seek it out.

What was she going to do?

The fireworks wouldn't start until it was dark. And, she

crossed the room to peek out her window, it was heading that way. She needed to get out to the viewing area. Tying her windbreaker around her waist, she tucked her phone into her pocket. She couldn't do anything about the sweatshirt now except pray Jake didn't notice it.

11

J ake grinned as Sean jogged up. "You ready?"

Sean dropped his sweatshirt on a log and rubbed his hands together. "You bet. What do you want me to do?"

"Come over here first, and I'll walk you through the system. After I took the licensing exams and got my pyrotechnician permit, I went on a shopping spree and ended up finding a fantastic deal on this guy." Jake patted the electronic firing system that he'd set up on a table and pointed to where the mortar racks were arranged down by the lake. "We'll load up the shells—that's what actually creates the fireworks—here in a minute. I've already run all the wires, but they're not connected. Once we're set, and it's dark, we'll run everything from back here. I've got enough racks that we won't have to reload. Safer that way."

"Cool."

Jake grinned. "Yeah."

"How come you got certified in this? It's not like it's a useful skill."

"Sure it is. It got me a summer camp position." Jake clapped Sean on the shoulder. "Mostly though? My friend, Gabe, does this big Christmas light display every year on his property. I was thinking it'd be fun to have fireworks on the weekend at closing time this year."

Sean nodded. "So you did this to help a friend out?"

"And to get to play with fireworks." Jake shrugged. "Do you really need more of an excuse than that?"

"Nope. This is cool." Sean's eyes shone with something Jake couldn't quite place, but it warmed his heart. "Thanks for letting me watch."

"Anytime. Now, unlike what I told your mom, you actually have to stay back here while I load everything up, but if you're super careful, I'll let you help carry the boxes down there."

Sean snorted. "Let me carry things? Gosh. Thanks."

"Come on." Jake pointed to a carton of mortars while bending to grab the larger one beside it.

Jake waited until Sean was back by the firing system before he began the somewhat tedious process of loading the shells into the mortars. There was a bit of science to the layout, only because it helped him make sure he hooked them up to the firing system in such a way that would get the show he envisioned. Not that if something went off at the wrong time it would be a disaster, but he wanted it to be perfect. To impress Deb.

He smiled and whispered yet another prayer of thanks to God for bringing her into his life. He'd never considered the idea of a ready-made family before, but Sean? The kid was amazing. Jake could love that boy as his own in a heartbeat. It was fast. Too fast, most likely. But that didn't change Jake's heart. He'd bide his time, figure out a way for them to continue to see each other after he went back to D.C. Five hours wasn't that far. At least, he didn't mind driving it. And his schedule at IA was flexible enough he could probably take Friday off fairly often and make it a three-day weekend.

Would she be willing to see where things went? That was

the conversation they needed to have. And since there were only four days of camp left, they needed to have it tonight.

Jake tucked the last shell into its mortar and double-checked the row. Everything looked good. He jogged back to the table where Sean waited. "Now we can hook up the wires to the firing console and we'll be ready."

"Can I help with this?"

"Sure. Look. I've laid them out in order, so we just work down the line." Jake demonstrated the process of sliding the wires into the alligator clips that connected them to the console. "You do one, I'll watch. If you've got it, then we can work both ends to the middle."

Sean had quick, nimble fingers. And he was a fast learner. Jake nodded. "All right, keep going. I'll work on this end."

It didn't take long with both of them working, which was good. Once the sun sank below the tree line, it started growing dark quickly. And the temperature started to drop. Jake quelled a shiver. At least he'd worn jeans, though he should've grabbed long sleeves. Oh well. It wouldn't take that long.

"Ready?" Jake pointed to the power switch. "Hit that puppy and we'll get the show on the road."

Sean reached for the switch. Jake snickered at the goose-bumps on the boy's arm.

"Dude. You brought a sweatshirt. Go put it on." Jake shook his head and flipped a few toggles to get the system ready. "All right...we're ready to go in three...two...one...let's do it."

Jake punched the first button and studied Sean as he returned, now clad in a grey sweatshirt with...was that his high school's crest? He squinted in the low light. It was. "Where'd you get that?"

Sean glanced down and shrugged. "It's my mom's. She has a ton of them 'cause she went to like three different high schools before her sophomore year. I think she left this one mid-year? Then she was homeschooled her junior and senior year."

Jake's mouth went dry. He pointed to the button that needed to get pushed and watched the mortars as Sean launched the explosive. Deb had gone to his high school? He scoured his memories for a student who left and could only come up with one, vague face. The same face he associated with the woman he'd slept with. But if he'd slept with Deb, that would mean...he turned to study Sean, his heart hammering in his chest.

Was it possible?

~

"THAT WAS INCREDIBLE. Our best fireworks display ever." Deb wound her arms around Jake's waist and squeezed.

Jake dragged her arms off him and stepped back. He reached down to grab the last mortar rack and sling it into the bed of his truck. Sean had helped with cleanup until it was time for lights out, then he'd gone to watch the cabin so Jake could finish up here. He'd hoped his blood would cool before Deb found him. So far that seemed like an impossibility.

"Jake? Did something go wrong?" Deb reached for him again.

"Were you ever going to tell me Sean is my son?"

Her jaw dropped and her eyes grew wide. Her breath came in short gasps. "What do you mean?"

He scoffed. He hadn't been positive. Not completely. But if that wasn't an admission, he wouldn't recognize one if he heard it. "I hoped you liked me—respected me—enough to be honest."

"Jake."

"Don't. Just don't, Deb. That sweatshirt? The one that was new my sophomore year? Our sophomore year?" He swallowed the bile crawling up his throat. Here in front of him was his biggest regret and instead of throwing himself on her mercy and begging forgiveness, he was as close to yelling as he'd been in a long time. Still, he couldn't get past one single fact: he had a son. Jake shook his head, his eyes burning, and walked to the driver's side of the truck. He should leave her. Let her walk back around to the main part of camp. Maybe she'd find the truth with some extended soul searching. Except...it was late, and dark. "You coming?"

JAKE STARED at the ceiling trying to solidify his thoughts into a coherent prayer, but the words wouldn't come. He'd confessed his sin. As soon as he'd found out, he'd confessed it. Rededicated his life to Christ—more like dedicated for the first time. For all that his parents had taken him to church his entire life, the words had only penetrated long enough for him to parrot them back when asked. Until he realized just how much his rebellion was costing. And it wasn't even him paying the price. That unnamed girl...Deb. It had been Deb.

He rolled over and buried his face in the pillow as a sob tore from his lungs. "Oh God...why? Why would you let this happen?"

There wasn't an answer. No booming voice from heaven. No soft, still whisper in his soul. Just the same searing pain that had been there before—a fire that raged with no hope of being extinguished.

12

———

Deb stood at the entrance to the main lodge with her clipboard and pen as parents moved in and out, collecting their campers. Jake hadn't spoken to her since he'd dropped her off on Monday night. Not that she'd made a ton of effort to reach out. What was she supposed to say? The truth was, no, she hadn't planned to tell him. Ever. He was leaving camp today and they lived miles—and worlds— apart. Had he really thought they had a chance for more?

She swallowed and blinked back tears. Now wasn't the time. This afternoon, once the campers were gone, before any new counselors checked in, she could get it all out of her system. Until then she would fake a smile and see everyone on their way.

"Mom?"

Her smile grew and she slipped an arm around Sean's waist. "Hi, sweetheart."

"What's going on with you and Jake?"

The smile faded. She glanced in Jake's direction and sighed. He was busy chatting with the parents of one of his campers. "Can we talk about this later?"

"Why? There's no one here. Most of the kids are gone. What'd you do?"

"What makes you think I did anything?"

"Come on, Mom. This is the first time you haven't had a litany of excuses to keep you from a second date—or even from going on the first one. You like him. But you haven't sat with him at a meal or looked his way, really, since Monday. You can say you're sorry, you know. Whatever you did, he'll probably forgive you. He's cool."

Deb closed her eyes and sent up a quick prayer for the right words. "It's more complicated than that."

Sean shook his head. "Why do adults always say that and yet, when I'm the one who messes up, you're quick to point out that all I have to do is apologize and ask forgiveness?"

Apologize and ask forgiveness. There was no way it would be that simple. She'd have to explain why she never contacted Jake—to him and to her parents. She'd have to admit to everyone—including herself—that she'd been the sexual aggressor. She'd known about his blackouts, the whole school did. It was a running joke, even among the unpopular kids. Maybe she hadn't known just how complete they were—she'd hoped he'd remember enough that he'd hang out with her afterward. When it was clear he didn't, moving had been a lot easier. It beat dealing with the shame that washed through her whenever she saw him in the halls. Worst of all? She'd have to share Sean. Jake would want that. He'd deserve that.

She couldn't do it.

"Don't worry about it, okay? We had a summer camp romance and now it's over. It happens." Deb squeezed him close until he pushed away.

"You just don't get it, do you Mom? It's not all about you. Not always. There are two of us in this family. And we both need a man in our life." Sean spun around and ran from the lodge.

Deb pressed a hand to her heart as he sprinted away. She was doing the best she could. Wasn't that enough?

It took several heartbeats for her to realize a family was talking to her. She'd completely missed what they said. Hopefully it was something positive about their child's experience. She forced a smile. "That's great. I'm so glad you could come. We'll look forward to seeing you again next year."

"Here are the keys to the range, the trail maps, and the key to the cabin. I took the linens off the bed and brought them to the lodge but there weren't fresh ones anywhere that I could find, so the counselor's bed is unmade." Jake extended the pile of camp items, his expression blank.

Deb cleared her throat, but the lump in it didn't budge. "That's okay. There's a cleaning crew that goes through today. They'll take care of it. We appreciate you taking the time to help out for this camp session. Maybe we'll see you back next year?"

His eyebrows shot up. "Nice speech. You're welcome. Or, well, the camp is welcome."

She winced. "Jake."

He shook his head. "I still can't talk to you, so just don't."

She sagged back into the desk chair. Jake was the last to check out. She'd hoped—planned—to try and talk to him. Explain...something. But how could she do that if he wouldn't listen? A tiny voice in her head called her a chicken. She'd made people hear her out before. But Jake...what was she supposed to say to him? The justifications she'd used over the years fell flat.

It didn't matter. He was gone now.

She tilted back so she could see out the window into the

parking lot. Jake stood at his truck, his hand on the handle of the door, talking to Sean. Her heart constricted.

Her son's hands flew in the air as he spoke—what was he lobbying for? The intense concentration was something she recognized from the many times through the years when he'd argued, convincingly most of the time, for one thing or another. It was how they'd ended up with a pet lizard. Deb couldn't suppress the shudder. That thing...was not a pet. And of course it didn't have the decency to run off or die like their less objectionable pets had.

Jake glanced over his shoulder and their eyes met for one long, searing second before he looked away. Deb's heart raced. Jake shook his head and patted Sean's shoulder. The boy flung his arms around Jake. After a moment, Jake wrapped his arms around Sean and rested his cheek on the boy's head.

A tear slipped down her cheek, followed by another. Deb wiped at them, blinking furiously. Jake turned and their eyes met again. This time, she looked away.

13

J ake dumped his duffel bag on the floor by the washing machine and glanced around his apartment. He'd lived here since the end of February and it still wasn't home. Every month when rent was due, the management company asked if he didn't want to switch to a one-year lease instead of paying the extra fee to keep it temporary. He was going to buy a house, though. Eventually. One where he could settle down and build a family.

Unbidden, an image of Sean, and then Deb, standing with him in front of a house formed in his mind. But that was never going to happen. Not now. But Sean...that was a possibility. He bent and unzipped the duffel and grabbed handfuls of clothes and dropped them in the washer. Jake added soap, spun the dial and hit start just as the buzzer for his door sounded.

He strode over and pulled it open. "Perfect timing...you're not the pizza guy."

Gabe chuckled. "Nope. But I figured there might be dinner in the offing, so I figured I'd swing by and welcome you home. I brought soda."

"All right, come in. I'll share my pie, but only because you brought something to drink. Why aren't you on a date?"

Gabe kicked the door closed behind him and ambled to the living room. He dropped onto the sofa and put his feet up on the plastic crate that stood in as an ottoman. "Tori's working a story and has interviews lined up tonight and most of tomorrow. In some ways it's nice—keeps me from having to hear her obsess over wedding choices. I mean, I get that it's a big deal, something we only do once. But how hard is it to make a decision on what shade of pink to use on the invitations?"

"Pink? Seriously?" Jake shook his head. Wasn't the guy supposed to at least get some input into these matters?

Gabe shrugged. "Apparently. I really don't care, so I told her whatever she wanted. So...pink it is. I did nix the bubblegum shade. She's looking at softer ones now. Some are so pale they're practically white."

"Do you even hear yourself?"

"Yes. Which is the other reason I'm over here."

Jake nodded. "Not a moment too soon, from the sound of it. We'll play something gory after we eat. Maybe pretending to be in the special forces will get you back to normal."

"One can hope." The buzzer sounded again and Gabe popped to his feet. "I'll get it. Consider it your welcome home present."

Jake yanked a bottle of soda out of the plastic rings and spun it open. This was exactly what he needed. The quiet evening with pizza and the television faded away, replaced by easy camaraderie. He hadn't realized he missed Gabe—and Rick, for that matter—until he'd showed up.

"Here we are. Toss one of those sodas this way, will you?" Gabe dropped the pizza box onto the crate and flipped the lid open. "Look at all that meat. You know how to order, man."

Jake stood and handed Gabe a drink. "I'll get plates. I've

graduated from super slob to semi-housetrained since leaving college, you know."

Gabe snickered. When Jake returned and handed him a plate, he pulled a slice free and took a bite. "Mmm. So, how was camp?"

Jake snagged his own slice. How much to say? He'd never hidden anything from Gabe and Rick—they were as close as brothers. Maybe closer. They knew about his drinking problem in high school as well as what had finally made him stop. And yet... "It was good. Mostly."

"Uh oh. The mostly have something to do with the camp director you mentioned? Oh, what was her name? Deb, right?"

Jake nodded as he chewed. He took a swig of soda to wash down the bite.

"Didn't work out?"

"It looked like it was going to. She's something special, man. Besides being interesting to talk to, we had chemistry."

"The combo of friendship and chemistry is hard to beat. What happened?"

Jake sighed and set his plate down on the floor, his appetite evaporating. "She's the one."

"Why is this a bad thing? The distance? You two can work that out."

"No. Not that kind of the one. The one. From high school."

Gabe's brows lifted. "Oh."

"Yeah. Oh."

"Wait. You mentioned she had a son. How old is he?"

"Fifteen." Jake waited as Gabe put the pieces together. "Exactly."

"You have a son."

"Yeah." Jake let out a long breath. "I have a son. And I'm not sure exactly what to do about it."

"Whoa. What'd she say when you asked her about it?" Gabe

finished his first slice of pizza and dragged a second onto his plate.

Jake twirled the soda bottle in his hands. "She wasn't going to tell me. I'd been thinking long term, already plotting how we might make things work and what it would take to get her to come up this way, but she was just waiting for me to leave so her secret would be safe."

"Ouch."

Jake set the bottle down and rubbed the back of his neck. "I think I'm going to see a lawyer. Sean—that's my boy—he's a great kid. I'm entitled to shared custody, aren't I?"

Gabe cleared his throat. "Are you sure you want to go that route? That sounds...like it would probably finish off any chance you might still have with Deb."

"What chance? She had plenty of time to explain. I figured it out on Monday after the fireworks. She hid away all week and barely said two words to me when it was time for me to leave. There's no chance there. All that's left is to make sure Sean gets an opportunity to know his father."

"Does he know about you?"

"I don't think so. Not given the way I found out. Plus, he made several comments that suggested his mom always told him she didn't know who his father was. But she knew. She admitted it when I asked."

Gabe puffed his cheeks out. "Wow. So...you want him to find out from a lawyer?"

"No. Deb will have to tell him, I guess."

"You don't think he'll be upset? I mean...you're going to effectively sue his mom, right?"

Jake's shoulders fell. He hadn't considered it from that angle. "If he doesn't want to spend time with me, I'll respect that. But don't you think he has the right to make that choice?"

Gabe shook his head. "I don't know. It sounds sticky, no matter what happens."

"So you don't think I should even talk to a lawyer?"

"Didn't say that. It probably doesn't hurt to talk. I'll text Shannon and see if she knows anyone. She seems to have contacts everywhere. Speaking of Shannon, did you know she's coming back to the office?"

"Really? Why?"

"The youngest starts Kindergarten in the fall. She doesn't want to be working from home with no one around who needs her. Plus, I think she's just ready to be back to full time. With the three of us back in the States, it'll be good to take the executive tasks off Angel's shoulders anyway, let her get back to being only front desk and occasional support."

That would be good. Angel was great at the front desk but had been clearly struggling to balance it all with all three of the bosses in town all the time. And Shannon was more than able to handle the three of them. "Cool. What else did I miss?"

JAKE LEANED BACK and crossed his legs. The weekend had sped by, as had a day back in the office. Shannon had come through with the name of a family law attorney and, surprisingly, he'd been able to get an appointment the next day. The receptionist looked up and smiled before returning to her computer. She'd assured him several times that Mr. Sommersby would be with him very soon, but still the minutes ticked by. Should he ask about rescheduling? They didn't need him in the office, but after being gone for three weeks, he wanted to be there.

A man opened the door behind the receptionist and shook the hand of the exiting client. "Mr. McGill? Thanks for waiting, come on back. Do you want some coffee or a soda?"

"I'm good, thanks." Jake stood and followed the attorney into his office. He sat in the chair indicated and took a deep breath to calm his racing heart. Why was it doing that? This was the right thing. Wasn't it?

"What brings you here today?"

"Well, Mr. Sommersby, it's like this." Jake ran through the basics of the situation with Deb and Sean. "I want to know my son. What can I do to make that happen?"

"Well, you can start by calling me Grant."

Jake smiled. "Okay."

"After that...are you sure you want to get the law involved? Have you tried talking to Ms. Magarry and reaching some kind of equitable solution?"

"I...don't see that happening. She admitted she had no plans to tell me Sean was my son. She's known...for fifteen years she's known and made no attempt to find me." That ate at his soul. He'd had no chance to do the right thing. No option. Well, he was going to do the right thing now, even if he had to force it on her.

"You realize if you prove paternity you'll be required to provide child support?"

Jake nodded. "That's fine."

Grant steepled his fingers. "Okay. I think the first step we ought to take is make contact and let her know that you're going to be pursuing visitation. That may be enough to get Ms. Magarry to negotiate with you without having to take anything to court. If not, the next step would be proving paternity. This is easily done through DNA, which the court can compel if it comes to that."

Jake closed his mouth on the objection he'd been about to make. He didn't think she'd submit voluntarily. It was good to know the court could make her. Something pinged at the back of his mind. Sean. What would Sean think of all this? He'd want this too, wouldn't he? Jake swallowed the lump in his throat.

"Once paternity is determined, then it's a matter of figuring out visitation. Again, it'll be easier if she agrees to negotiate. Her attorney will likely encourage her to do just that. But if it has to go to court, the process could take a while and be stressful for everyone involved." Grant held Jake's gaze. "So you need to be sure you want to proceed before we get started."

Jake sighed. "You don't think I should."

Grant pursed his lips. "I didn't say that."

"Not in so many words."

"I'm not convinced this is the best way to go about it. I've seen case after case—no, nothing exactly like this, but there are enough similarities—where things turn ugly and no one is happy at the end. You can get exactly what you want and still be disappointed."

Jake nodded. "I...can see that."

"Do you know for certain that the boy, Sean was it? Is going to be happy about this? Will he embrace it as a chance to get to know his dad, or will he see it as you harassing his mother?"

"I'm not sure."

"Don't you think you should be, before you get started?"

Probably. He let out a deep breath. He needed to do more praying about this. "I guess you're right. You're not exactly what I expected. Aren't attorneys supposed to encourage you to hire them?"

Grant grinned. "Not the good ones."

"So?" Rick shifted away from his monitor to meet Jake's gaze.

"I don't know. I'm going to pray more. Or, more truthfully, start praying about it. I've been running on hurt and anger. I haven't put a lot else into it."

Rick nodded. "I can understand that. Sounds like it's good you went to the guy you went to."

"Yeah. Shannon's recommendation. How about you? How are you and Annabelle doing?"

Rick grinned. "She's amazing. I think we've decided on September for the wedding. I was hoping you and Gabe would stand up with me. You will, right?"

"Wouldn't miss it for the world. That's great, man. Which of us gets to be Best Man?"

"Ha. I'm not falling for that. And also, you should know that was exactly Gabe's question. You're just going to have to settle for being groomsmen. Or I'll have two best men. Whichever way you want."

Jake chuckled. "Just giving you a hard time. When you have a firm date, make sure I get it so I can put...September? Dude, that's soon."

"Yeah. Annabelle's trying to get the church. Labor Day was our initial thought, but that's been booked for months. She's throwing herself at the mercy of the church secretary today to see what we can get. Once we have a date it's going to be a rush to get invitations out, but we aren't planning on a huge wedding. Annabelle's parents are determined to throw a big shindig for the reception though. There was no talking them out of it."

"Aw, poor baby. Where are they having it?"

"Dunno yet. It'll depend on the date. I'm guessing it's going to be somewhere downtown. They love hobnobbing with the big wigs in D.C. Annabelle didn't fight too hard on the reception, since that meant her parents let go of having a huge society ceremony. Anyway, start thinking about who you'll bring."

"Bring? Can't I just come alone? I'll get paired up with a bridesmaid, right?"

Rick shook his head. "I think it's just going to be Tori. And I'm pretty sure Gabe is going to want her to hang with him. You need a date."

Jake sighed. In an alternate universe, he'd have Deb. Now? "I'll see what I can do."

Rick clapped him on the shoulder. "Cheer up. You've got at least two months."

Two months. Two years. It wasn't likely to matter. The only woman he wanted on his arm wanted nothing to do with him.

14

How was it already the end of July? Deb hit send on the final checkout report for the camp and leaned back in her desk chair. The campers were gone. The counselors were packing up, though all were officially checked out. Sean was helping close the pool and then he'd come here. She'd already loaded their car and the paperwork was done. Camp was officially over.

They'd asked her to come back next year as Camp Director.

Mrs. Beech had decided she was getting too old to keep doing it.

Had she enjoyed it? It was...different than being a counselor. Considerably less free time, but the same sense of accomplishment, of mattering. She didn't have to tell them right away. They'd said she could wait as long as October before they'd have to start advertising the position. Who knew camp director positions took so long to fill? She'd talk it over with Sean, see what he had to say about it. Would he want to come next year? She kept expecting him to say he was too old. The Counselor-in-Training program was a good thing, but at some point, wouldn't he rather they traveled?

She sighed. Travel. It was one of the few things she really wanted to do, but at the same time, was scared of. She'd spent so much time moving as a child that being in one place, knowing that she had roots planted and that those roots had a good chance to dig deep...she couldn't put a price on it. But was she doing the right thing by Sean? Jake would probably be all about the travel.

Jake.

Why did she keep thinking about him? They'd done just fine without him for fifteen years, so why, now that he was gone, did it seem like there was a huge hole in her life? And Sean...what was she supposed to do? Tell him the truth?

The truth shall set you free.

Sure...but free from what? Independence? A son who loved and respected her? Sean would hate her. Would he want to go spend time with Jake without her? She'd have to let him go eventually. College wasn't that far off. But...she blew out a breath. Maybe Jake would just let it go. She laughed. Right.

"What's funny?" Sean tromped through the door and dropped a backpack on the floor as he sat.

"Nothing. You all set?"

"Yep. Pool's closed, I double checked the boys' cabins on my way past and they're all clear. When can we go?"

"I'm all set. We just have to stop at the office on our way down the mountain to turn in the keys. I don't know if they have someone else using the camp for August. They told me to leave it the way we found it, so I think we're square. Your grandparents called and wanted to know if you were interested in taking a trip up to D.C. next week."

He brightened. "Yeah? That'd be cool. Do you think we could look Jake up and say hi?"

"Honey."

Sean scowled. "You don't miss him at all?"

"I do. It's just...complicated. Plus, I'm not sure your grandparents invited me." Deb forced a smile. They did this every summer, thinking she needed a vacation from being a mom before school started back up. It was the loneliest week of the year.

He sighed.

"Does that mean you don't want to go?"

"Nah. I'll go. D.C. is always fun. And you need a break before you have to report for school anyway. How long?"

"We can find out tonight at dinner. They're taking us out for steak. Grandma said something about how she knows we only eat pasta at camp. I tried to explain that the food here was actually pretty good. But you know how she gets."

"Even if I didn't, I wouldn't say no to steak." Sean grinned.

"All right. Let's go." Deb stood, checked the drawers of the desk one last time, and grabbed her purse and an enormous ring of keys off the top of the desk.

"Mom. Would you be mad if I asked grandma and grandpa about looking Jake up?"

She sighed. "Let me think about it. Okay?"

DEB STRETCHED out on the lounge chair on the deck. It was good to be home. Her parents had been thrilled to see Sean again. And her. Probably. But they doted on their grandson in ways they'd never doted on her. Now, Sean was tucked in his bed asleep. She'd already been in to peek at him. That was something she missed at camp—the chance to simply stand and watch his chest rise and fall and revel in the miracle that was her son.

A tear slipped down her cheek.

He was her world. Maybe he wasn't what she'd planned, but Sean was a blessing straight from God. Did she have any right to deny that blessing to Jake?

She picked her cell phone up from where she'd set it on the deck and, after taking a deep breath, tapped Jake's number.

"Hello?"

"Hi, Jake. It's Deb. Deb Magarry?"

"Yeah, I got that. What's up?" His voice was brisk, but not hostile. She'd take that as a sign that maybe, just maybe, there was a way to do this without it being ugly.

Deb cleared her throat. "First I wanted to apologize. I haven't handled this whole situation well at all."

"When you say 'this whole situation,' what exactly are you referring to? Camp? Or the last fifteen years?"

Okay. So he wasn't going to make it easy. That figured. "I was thinking camp. But...you're not wrong."

He grunted.

"Look. I wanted to talk to you about Sean."

His voice softened. "Yeah? What about him?"

Deb swallowed. "He's going to D.C. with his grandparents next week. He asked if I'd mind if he looked you up. He...really connected with you at camp. Would...would it be okay if he came to see you? Do you have time?"

"I do. Give him my number and we'll work it out." His breath crackled in the phone. "I should tell you, I've spoken to an attorney. I want to know my son. To spend time with him, if it's what he wants."

She closed her eyes, her stomach knotting. He'd contacted an attorney? She couldn't lose Sean. "You can't...you don't need to take me to court. Why...I don't understand."

"That makes two of us. You kept him from me, Deb. I never knew, never had even the slightest idea. Why wouldn't you tell me? Do you have any idea the guilt and shame I've lived with for fifteen years? To think I slept with someone and was so drunk I had no idea? And then to find out I fathered a child?" Jake's voice broke. "What else was I supposed to do?"

What would she have done in his place? Would she have acted any differently if their roles were reversed? She hoped not. It said so much about his character that he wanted to know Sean, to do right by him. Even if it hurt and scared her. "I don't know. I'll...talk to Sean and my parents before they go. Tell them the whole story."

"Thank you."

She ended the call and stared unseeing into the night as tears dripped down her cheeks.

DEB TWISTED her fingers in her lap and studied her son. What was this going to do to their relationship? Her gaze darted over to her parents. They...would stand by her. They always had. But Sean? Her heart ached. This was the one thing she'd wanted to avoid. Was it like ripping off a bandaid? Better to just do it fast? She cleared her throat. "I haven't been completely honest with you."

"With me?" Sean furrowed his brow. "Really, mom?"

She rubbed a hand over her heart. "All of you. But maybe you, most of all. I know—have always known—who your father is."

"What?" Her dad jumped to his feet, scowling. "Deborah Magarry, I have half a mind to turn you over my knee. I don't care if you are thirty years old. That boy has some answering to do."

"No, Dad. He doesn't. And that's the reaction that kept me from saying anything." She took a deep breath and explained about Jake's drinking problem, how it was well known that he had blackouts at parties. She mentioned her crush on him, her desire to be accepted by the popular crowd by doing something no one else had managed yet. "I liked him. Even though he had no idea who I was, or what he was doing."

"Why tell us now?" Her mother leaned forward, elbows on her knees, a puzzled look on her face.

This was it. She wiped damp palms on her pants and swallowed. "Because he's asked to spend some time with Sean."

"How did he even find out about me? Who is he? I don't want to be forced to see some guy just because he's overcome with guilt now for some stupid reason." Sean crossed his arms, a frown etched on his face.

"It's Jake, sweetheart. Jake is your biological father."

Sean's eyes widened and his arms slipped down to his side. "Jake? Camp Jake?"

She nodded, tears burning the back of her eyes.

"When...when did he find out?" Sean's voice was hoarse.

"You wore my sweatshirt to the fireworks. He asked me about it later that night." Deb hugged her arms around herself to ward off the sudden chill.

Sean nodded. "When he stopped wanting to be with you."

"No. It wasn't him, honey. It was me. I was trying to protect you."

Sean shook his head.

"Oh, Deborah. Why wouldn't you say something when we asked?" Her mother grabbed her father's hand. Dad looked like he was ready to murder someone. Whether it was Jake or her was up in the air.

Deb shrugged. "There didn't seem to be a point. We'd moved. And I knew he had no idea what had happened—or it was likely he didn't, at least. Why would I do that to him?"

"He might have persuaded you to place for adoption." Her dad shook his head. "That's what you were most worried about. You never did want to even consider giving Sean up. Now...well, now I can't say I blame you. But back then I sure never understood."

Was that part of it? Deb dragged her lower lip between her teeth. It might be. She'd never been able to give the right amount of consideration to adoption. She believed in it. Wholeheartedly. Even at fifteen she had. But not for this baby. Not for Sean. Thankfully her parents had been willing to walk alongside her when she didn't choose what they wanted. "I'm so sorry."

Sean scoffed.

It was a knife to Deb's heart. Tears filled her eyes. "I'm not sorry about you. I could never be sorry about you, Sean. You have to know that."

He gave a curt nod, then stood. "I'm going to go pack."

Deb's shoulders sank along with her heart. "I'll text you Jake's number."

Her parents stayed while Sean strode from the room. Deb prayed that they would be gentle. She couldn't take another punch to the gut like the one Sean had just given.

Disappointment and anger pumped off her father's every move. Her mother made little soothing motions that were almost as heartbreaking.

"I'm sorry, Daddy."

"You said that already. Any other lies you need to get off your chest?"

"Honey." Her mother frowned.

Deb flinched, the verbal hit leaving a bruise to her heart. Her voice was a strained whisper. "No."

Her dad studied her for several heartbeats before he stood with a brusque nod. "We'll be by for Sean in the morning."

Mom opened her mouth then sighed. She offered a timid, bolstering smile before following Dad.

Deb buried her face in her hands and let the tears fall. *God? I was doing the best I could. I know I wasn't where you wanted me to be back then, but I am now, aren't I? Please...*She didn't know how to finish the prayer. Hopefully, God understood.

15

"Hi, Jake."

Jake pushed away from the table in the middle of the Ballston Mall's food court and stood, offering his fist for a bump. "Sean. Good to see you, man."

Sean hesitated before bumping Jake's fist, then he threw his arms around Jake and squeezed.

Jake swallowed the lump in his throat and wrapped his arms around the boy. He'd wondered if things would be weird now that Sean knew he was his father. Apparently not. He glanced over Sean's head at the sound of someone clearing their throat and froze. "You want to introduce me to your grandparents?"

Sean stepped back, a huge grin splitting his face. "Sure. This is my grandma and grandpa. Grandma, Grandpa, this is Jake."

Chuckling, Jake extended his hand. "Mr. and Mrs. Magarry. I'm Jake McGill."

Mrs. Magarry's hand trembled in his.

Mr. Magarry's grip was firmer than was strictly polite.

Jake looked at Sean. "Where do you want to grab lunch?"

"Can grandma and grandpa eat with us? They said they'd like to get to know you a little."

"Of course." Jake's voice remained steady, though his heart thundered in his chest. He met Mr. Magarry's eyes. "Is there a particular food choice you'd prefer, Sir? Or there are a couple of sit-down restaurants on the other side of the mall."

"We can let Sean choose. He knows what we like." Mr. Magarry pulled out a chair for his wife. "We'll hold the table."

Okay. This wasn't going at all like Jake had imagined. What had he expected? That they'd throw their arms open and welcome him to the family like Sean had? Maybe it's what he hoped for, but the reality was much more reasonable. Cold and distant. He tried to put himself in their place...and yeah, that's probably how he'd act, too. He turned to smile at Sean. "All right, lead on."

Sean grinned and stuffed his hands in his pockets. When they were on the other side of the food court, he stopped in front of a sandwich shop. "We can get something for my grand-parents here. Can I go somewhere else though?"

"Sure." Jake reached for his wallet. "It's the food court, that's why there are so many options, right?"

"Right." Sean studied the menu above the heads of the workers. His voice was nearly a whisper when he added, "Is it weird?"

Jake cocked his head to the side. "Is what weird?"

"Knowing that I'm your kid?" He turned and looked at Jake. "Are you disappointed?"

Jake vigorously shook his head. "Not in you. In myself, in your mom. But not in you."

"Do you hate her?"

Did he? Jake scrubbed a hand over his face. "I wanted to. But no, I don't hate her. I just wish...never mind. Let's order those sandwiches."

Sean frowned but turned back to the food stall.

What was he thinking, nearly telling a teen that he was half in love with Deb? There was no future for them, she'd made that clear. And even though the month since camp ended had done nothing to lessen the feelings he'd started to have for her, it was pointless. He needed to focus on the positive: he was getting a chance to know Sean. Maybe that would be enough. It would have to be.

JAKE SAT out on what passed for the balcony of his apartment. Sean and his grandparents had come to the office after lunch and taken a tour of the open areas. Mr. and Mrs. Magarry had seemed impressed when they realized Jake was one of the founders. Not enough to ask him to use their first names, but they'd stopped glaring at him. He'd tried to explain that he hadn't known. That now he did know, he was trying to do the right thing. But he got the distinct impression they weren't convinced him being in Sean's life was the right thing.

He huffed out a breath. It was time to make the call he'd been dreading since he found out. He picked up his cell and stared at it. Was his high school behavior ever going to stop causing his mom pain? He punched the number and waited as it rang.

"Jake? Baby, it's Tuesday. You don't usually call during the week. Is everything okay?"

He smiled and a quiet chuckle escaped. "Hi, Mom. I can't just call because I feel like it?"

"You can. Of course you can. You usually don't though."

That was fair. He should try and do better. He loved his parents, even though it was also a good thing they weren't local. Time and distance had done a lot to help their relationship. And now...he was probably going to ruin it all over again. He cleared his throat. "As it happens, I have some news."

"Oh? Hang on, I'll get Dad." She hollered for his father and Jake held the phone away from his ear. Did she even try to cover the mouthpiece?

His dad's grumbling got closer. "What is it, dear? I had to pause my show. You know I hate that."

"It's Jake. He says he has news. Maybe he's finally found a nice girl. Be good. Here, let me put it on speaker." Several beeps blared in Jake's ear before his mother spoke again. "There. We're both here, honey. Go ahead."

"Hi, Jake. Make it fast, I have my show paused."

Jake laughed at the mental picture of his parents sitting around the kitchen table. His father's irritated scowl a direct contrast to his mother's expectant smile. Neither of them would be happy. *A little help, Lord? Please?* "Hi, Dad. I'll try. So...you remember my first two years of high school?"

His father snorted. "Son, your mother and I do. Do you?"

Jake winced.

"Harry. Jake, you don't listen to him. We've forgiven you. More importantly, Jesus has. And you're back walking with the Lord now. Unless...oh, no, are you drinking again? You know you just can't do that. Not with how your body reacts. I think I have the number of the counselor you saw in high school. He might not be practicing anymore though. Hmm. Let me think. Do you remember the name of that man at church, Harry, the one—"

"Mom. Stop. I'm not drinking." Jake scrubbed a hand over his face. This was going worse than he'd figured. And he hadn't had high hopes.

"You're not? Then why did you say you were? Honestly."

"He didn't, Marge. Let the boy talk. What about high school now, Jake?"

Leave it to Dad to get things back on track. "I never told you all of what factored in to me giving up drinking."

"That's fine, dear. We don't need details. We're just glad

you're okay." If his mom had been in the room with him, she would've been patting his arm.

Maybe the slow introduction was the wrong approach. "I have a son."

There was a long, ragged silence before anyone spoke.

"Say it again, Jake. I don't think your mom or I heard that right."

Jake swallowed. "I said, 'I have a son.' He's fifteen. I just found out about him this summer."

His mother burst into tears.

Jake closed his eyes. He'd broken her heart. Again. He could try and pretend it wasn't his fault, but that was a lie. More than anyone—even Deb—he was to blame. If he hadn't taken such pride in getting drunk like that...

"I'm sorry. I know it doesn't help."

There was a beep and his mother's sobs faded. "I moved to the other room, away from your mother. You understand this is a bit of a shock."

"I do. For me, too, Dad."

His dad scoffed. "I bet. Will we get to meet him, your boy?"

"Sean. His name's Sean. And I hope so. I'm going to try to arrange that. Dad...I told Deb, that's his mom, that I wanted to pursue custody. To be responsible for him. Not just because it's the right thing to do, but because he's a great kid. But is it? Is it the right thing to do?"

Harry grunted and the old leather recliner that was his father's standard position after supper squeaked as he settled in it. "Why wouldn't it be?"

"I spent the day with him, and his grandparents, today. And...I don't know. They're a unit, a family. Should I really be barging in on that just because I found out that I'm Sean's father?"

"She didn't tell you, then? She—what's her name, Deb?— wasn't trying to force you to help out?"

Jake sighed and related the story of how he'd figured it out. How Deb had never planned to let him know. "I was so angry. I spoke to a lawyer, was considering taking her to court. Then she called because Jake was coming up this way and wanted to see me. She wanted to know if it was okay. I...made her tell him. And her parents. Maybe that was wrong."

"There's more to this. You have feelings for her, don't you?"

Did he? "I don't want to."

His dad's belly laugh eased something in Jake's shoulder. "Boy, loving a woman has nothing to do with wanting to."

"I thought love was a choice. Isn't that what you and Mom always told me? That I should choose wisely?"

"True. We did. And it's still true. But sometimes, the one you choose to love is the one you don't always want to love cause she's done something that made you angrier than you've ever been in your life."

Deb had certainly done that. But that didn't mean he loved her. "I don't know, Dad."

"Let me tell you something. Maybe you're not all the way in love with her, but I can hear how close you are. Right now, temper might be clouding your judgment so you can't see it, but if you're asking my opinion, you need to figure out a way have that boy and his momma in your life on a permanent basis."

Jake blew out a breath. "I don't know if that's even possible."

"We'll pray for you. Our God is a God of the impossible."

"Thanks, Dad. Is Mom going to be okay?"

"Yeah. Don't you worry about her. I'll let her know she's going to have a daughter-in-law and grandson soon enough."

"Dad..."

"Don't try to make God smaller than he is. How many different summer camps did you look at? And apply to?"

"I don't know, five?"

"How many people even followed up with you?"

"Just the one."

"That's God at work. Trust in Him."

"It was nice of your grandparents to let you have dinner with me alone." Jake slid a menu across the table to Sean. The burger joint wasn't too crowded on a Wednesday night, but there were still very few empty tables.

"Yeah. I think they were happy to go back to the hotel and rest. We did a lot of walking today. I think Mom convinced them that this had to be an educational trip, they usually let me choose one or two museums and then we just kind of amble. Today it was like they were determined to see every room on every floor and read every word of the displays."

Jake chuckled. "Where?"

"Air and Space. I think they're planning on the National Gallery tomorrow." Sean made a gagging motion.

"It's not that bad. There's some beautiful stuff in there. I like to go down there after work sometimes, if I get away before they close."

"Really?"

"Really. Art isn't for sissies. You know that, right?"

Sean shrugged.

The server came over and took their orders, disappearing with the menus when she was done.

"You looking forward to school starting back up?"

Another shrug. "I guess. It's school, you know. You have to go."

Jake angled his head and frowned. "I thought I remembered you liking school. That's what you said at camp."

Sean sighed. "I do. I just...don't wanna look like a nerd. Not to you."

"Sean, I don't want you to be anyone other than yourself.

You're a great kid. I told your mom that several times at camp, long before I knew you were mine."

"You were just trying to get her to like you."

Jake scoffed. "I'm not clever enough to try that. I wanted her to like me because I like her. A lot. I think that ship has probably sailed though."

"Why?"

"She's mad that she has to share you. I think she's scared I'm going to try and take you away. And maybe there's a little guilt that she wasn't honest with me from the start."

"I hate her."

"Oh, Sean. You can't mean that. She's your mom. And sure, I think you and I both wish she'd done things differently, but she didn't. We have to work with what we have and forgive the missteps that were taken. And, beyond that, at the risk of being a broken record, she's your mom. You need to respect her."

"I guess." The beginnings of a sullen pout pulled at the edges of his mouth. "You still like her, even though she kept me from you?"

"I do. I really do." Jake leaned back as the server brought their orders to the table. When she was gone, he shook his napkin out and laid it in his lap. "I don't suppose you have any thoughts on how I might get her to like me back?"

16

Deb smiled at her department chair across the table. "This is just what I needed. Thanks for inviting me. With Sean gone with his grandparents all week, it's been lonely."

Peter leaned forward, the candlelight causing his front teeth to gleam. "I'm glad you were free. I'm looking forward to school starting myself."

"I haven't gotten my schedule yet, have you? I'm used to receiving it before the school year ends, but this year...I guess with Mr. Rumburger and his secretary retiring things in the front office got confused." She fidgeted. Why was Peter looking at her like that? Maybe she shouldn't have come after all. Candlelight? Should she make a comment about appreciating his friendship, emphasis on friend?

"Actually, I've had mine. I've been trying to get in touch with you all summer."

She frowned. There weren't any messages on voice mail at home. And he hadn't called her cell. "I go to camp every summer, you know that. But my parents always have my contact information if you lose it."

"Yes, well. I thought it was important to meet in person. You see, with Rumburger gone, they've asked me to transition to Principal. I've been looking to move to administration for years, but in a town this small, well, there aren't a ton of opportunities."

"That's great, Peter. I'm sure you'll do well. But what does this—"

"Since I'm moving up, we'll need a new department chair for math."

Her heart sped up. She'd love the challenge of department chair. What an opportunity! But she shouldn't act too excited. Peter was known for expecting women to be demure. The women at school played the game when he was around and rolled their eyes behind his back. Oh, geez. If he was principal, was he going to try and make them all wear skirts? He couldn't do that, could he? Best not to worry about that now, she'd organize a trip to the school board herself if he tried though. "Of course."

"I've asked Daniel to take on that position. And he has some, let's say reservations, about continuing to work with you."

Daniel? The guy who'd just finished his first year out of school, that Daniel? It had to be. There weren't any other Daniels, but...he had reservations about working with her? After she'd, essentially, had to do all his lesson planning the first semester to show him how? "I'm...not sure I understand. *Daniel* is the new department chair?"

Peter nodded, smiling. "I feel he's earned the chance. He had such a smooth first year—did you get a look at his lesson plans?"

Deb scoffed. "Of course I did. When I helped him write them."

"See, this is what he was afraid of. He mentioned that he

worried you would try to besmirch his reputation, say he was unqualified."

"He *is* unqualified! I've been at this school—in this department—for five years. He's fresh out of college and I'm not convinced he actually did any student teaching. But even if we pretend that Daniel's qualified, I have seniority."

Peter reached out and patted her arm. "I realize that. Which is why I thought I'd take you out tonight and see if you'd like to move up to the front office with me."

Deb inhaled deeply. Front office? Was the assistant principal leaving, too? She'd not heard anything about that, though if he got passed over and they put Peter in as principal, she couldn't blame him. "I'm listening."

"As you know, every principal is only as good as their admin. And you're incredibly organized and capable. You'd do a fine job. Plus, we'd get to see each other for the bulk of every day. I know that you feel the same pull I do. It's obvious. So, as my admin, we could see where things led."

Deb blinked, her mind reeling. This couldn't be happening. "I see. And if I'm not interested in stepping away from using my teaching credentials?"

He frowned as if the idea that she wasn't jumping at his offer had never occurred as a possibility. "I'm afraid Daniel was adamant that you couldn't be in his department. So, continuing as a math teacher isn't really an option at this juncture."

She pushed away from the table and stood, clasping her hands together to keep them from shaking. "I'm fairly certain what you're doing here isn't legal. I'll be speaking with an attorney and will get back to you next week."

"Don't be like that. This is a beautiful opportunity for you. Everyone agrees that I'm quite a catch. As a single mother, what options, really, do you have?"

Deb jerked her arm away from Peter's grasp and spun on

her heel. They couldn't do this. There was no way this was legal. And if Peter thought he could, he had another think coming. Her father had friends on the School Board, had considered running for a position at one point. She tried not to bother her parents when they left town—particularly when they had Sean with them. But tonight...well, she needed to talk to her dad.

"YOU DIDN'T HAVE to come home early. I'm so sorry, Sean." Deb reached for his duffel bag.

He tugged it away. "I got it. And yeah, we did. I can't believe that guy. What a jerk."

"My sentiments exactly." Her dad offered a tight smile and patted her shoulder. "Before I start making some phone calls, I want to say that Jake is an amazing young man. I'm glad he's going to be in your life. Now, I'm going to take your mom home and get on the phone. I'll let you know when I have some news."

"Thanks, Dad." Deb absently kissed her father's cheek, still lost in the idea of having Jake in her life. He wasn't going to be in her life. That caused a sharp pang. But it was true. Maybe he'd be in Sean's life, if they could work something out. But hers? Her lips tingled as she recalled their kisses on the steps of his cabin at camp. So what if they had chemistry? What did they have other than that? Fifteen years of lies. And a son.

Deb tracked Sean down in the laundry room where he was dumping his clothes into the washer. "So you had fun?"

"Yeah. D.C. is always cool."

It was like pulling teeth. "And Jake?"

Sean jerked his shoulder. "What about him?"

"How is he? Did you have fun? Was it weird?" Deb tucked her hands in the pockets of her jeans. "Or whatever. You don't have to talk about it if you don't want to."

He shook his head. "He's fine. Yes, we had fun. No. Surprisingly not. Geesh. The two of you are a pair. All he wanted to talk about was you, too."

She fought a grin. He'd asked about her? Warmth spread through her. Maybe...no. There was no maybe. How could he possibly forgive her? On the other hand, it sounded like Sean had. Or was trying to. "Mmmhmm. Why don't I believe that?"

"Whatever, Mom. Call him and ask if you don't believe me. I'm gonna go read. I haven't finished all my summer reading yet. Assuming we're still here, I'll have to get that done before school starts."

"Wait. What do you mean, 'assuming we're still here'? Why wouldn't we be here?"

"I dunno. We only have one high school. If you're not teaching there, wouldn't we have to move?"

"Oh, I'll be teaching there. Don't underestimate your grandfather." She ruffled his hair, laughing when he groaned and smoothed it back into place. "Are we okay, Sean?"

He nodded. "I guess."

"I love you. You know that, right?"

"Yeah. I love you, too."

"You're not mad still?" Deb bit the inside of her cheek. She was pushing, but she needed to know things were okay between them.

Sean sighed. "Maybe a little. But Jake said I needed to get over it. Work with what we had instead of wishing things were different. So I'm trying."

Jake said that? He'd stood up for her? She gave a slight smile. "All right. Go read."

"Sure. Go call Jake." He disappeared into his room.

Call Jake? No. That wasn't likely to happen. Maybe she'd just...her cell rang. Could her dad have gotten a hold of someone so quickly? She raced for where she'd set it to charge and was out of breath when she answered. "Hello?"

"Hi. Deb? You okay? It's Jake."

She let out a strangled laugh. Of course it was. Why was her heart racing? "Yeah. Yeah, I'm fine. I was running for the phone is all. What can I do for you?"

"Mostly checking to make sure everyone got home okay."

"Oh. Yeah, they're home. Did you want to talk to Sean? I can get him."

"I'll call him later. I really wanted to talk to you. How are you holding up?"

"What do you mean?"

"Your parents mentioned what that slime was trying to do. That's got to be frustrating."

That was an understatement. More...he really sounded like he cared. "I'm pretty confident Dad will get it figured out. At least, that's what I'm praying for. I can't afford to be unemployed. I know God will provide. Sometimes it's hard to remember."

"Hey. It's going to be all right. Even if you can't see it now. Have you ever considered moving?"

"Moving? I...no. No, it's safe here. It's home. I couldn't uproot Sean. He'd hate that." She rubbed her arms to fight off a sudden chill.

"Would he? I think you might be surprised."

She ran a hand through her hair. Was she supposed to consider moving? Uproot herself and Sean? What about her parents? Would they come? Of course they wouldn't. They'd retired here on purpose. "Where would we go? I couldn't go far...my parents..."

"Is D.C. too far?"

D.C.? She'd be near Jake. *Sean* would be near Jake. She wasn't interested for herself. Maybe enough reminders would make it true. "What are you saying?"

"I want you in my life, Deborah."

"Sean. You want Sean in your life." That's what he meant. It was all he could possibly mean.

"No. I want you."

"Why?" Her voice was barely a whisper. "After all I've done, why would you still want me? Why would ever forgive me?"

"I'm not perfect either. If I hadn't been the rebellious drunk I was...none of this would have happened. I don't know why you'd give me another chance. But I really, really want you to."

"It's because of Sean. You don't have to do this just because of Sean."

"I started falling for you before I knew Sean was mine. What I know now doesn't change anything."

How? "You were so angry at camp. What happened?"

"I talked to my dad. He...offered some perspective. And I've been praying about it—practically non-stop—since I got home."

She sighed. That was a lot of praying. More than she'd been doing. "I don't know what to say."

"Say you'll think about it?"

"Yeah. Okay."

"I'll call you later? Or you can call me when you've talked to your dad?"

"Sure. Good night, Jake."

Deb set the phone down and stared out the window into the rapidly darkening night. Her perfectly planned life was crumbling before her eyes. *Now what, God? Now what?*

17

J ake set his phone down and let out a breath. He'd put it all on the line. She hadn't jumped at it. But she hadn't laughed in his face and told him to leap off a cliff, either. So he'd call it a win. Or at least a tie. Her words pierced his heart. Why would she think she didn't deserve his forgiveness? Nobody deserved forgiveness...that's what made it special.

He searched his memories for some inkling of who Deb had been in high school. Sophomore year. Jake frowned. He'd had a massive crush on a girl that year—what was her name? It was one of those things that, at the time, had made him believe in love at first sight. Of course, he'd been too much of a dork to do anything about it. For all he hung out with the popular kids, that was just because they liked having him at their parties. He'd been quiet at heart, only talking to the girls who sought him out or his friends pushed his way. The ones who thought the bluster and macho of insecure boys was something to chase after.

Did he still have his yearbooks? They'd be in a box...where? Maybe in the closet? He'd stuffed a pile of boxes from his parents' house in there when he'd moved in. When he came back from Germany, they'd decided he was old enough to get his junk out of their house. He smiled. Mom had offered to hold it a little longer, but Dad wasn't having it.

Jake flipped on the light and eyed the stack of boxes. They were labeled in his mom's handwriting. Ah...there. He tugged the third box in the stack free, narrowly avoiding tipping the others over on top of himself. It was heavy. Maybe the year-books really were in here.

Back in the living room, Jake flipped open the lid and laughed. Staring up at him was a comic he'd made when he was supposed to be studying. It had all his teachers dressed as super heroes standing around a coffee pot. He pulled it out and set it aside. He hadn't drawn in years...maybe that'd be some inspiration to take it up again. Programs from school concerts, a boutonniere from some dance or other, and a basketball jersey were next and then, there they were: his yearbooks.

He found the one from sophomore year and flipped to the picture section. He skimmed through the pages, stopping occasionally to tap the photo of a friend and laugh at the memories. There was the girl he'd had a crush on. He flicked his gaze over to the names and shook his head. Unbelievable. His heart hammered in his chest. Wiping his suddenly clammy palms on his pants, he traced the name with a finger. She'd gone by Debbie back then. And no one was going to believe that he'd had a crush on her. He'd only told Jimmy, his best friend and captain of the basketball team. In fact, they'd been at Jimmy's house for the last party...had Jimmy put her up to it? Maybe he thought he'd be doing Jake a favor?

Crazy.

He'd had serious girlfriends in college, but there was always something missing. Nothing had compared to that high school crush. And now? Deb haunted his dreams. Was there any way to convince her that his feelings were completely about her, not some misplaced guilt about Sean?

Prayer. That's what his dad had recommended. And now that he was older, he recognized that most of the time, his dad was right.

JAKE DRUMMED his fingers on his desk. He had ten minutes until a big meeting with a new potential customer. His presentation of what IA could do for them was ready to go. Gabe and Rick had taken them to lunch before the meeting to schmooze. Jake could've gone but...that wasn't really his skill set. Plus this way he'd have the conference room ready to go. Still, he had a few minutes. He tugged his phone from his pocket and tapped a quick text to Sean.

How's your mom? Any word?

Deb hadn't called since they'd spoken on Saturday. Surely something had happened on Monday that was worth mentioning? It couldn't take as long for the wheels of bureaucracy to turn in a small town as it did in a large one, could it? His blood began to heat. The nerve of that jerk...he took a deep breath. It wouldn't serve any purpose to get all worked up before this meeting. His phone buzzed.

OK. Gpa got his friends working on it. Everyone freaked mom might leave. Ppl <3 her.

He smiled even as his heart began to ache. People love her. 'Cause she's good at what she does. He wanted her to have that recognition, for people to rally behind her. And then he wanted her to leave anyway. He typed a quick reply.

Good. Let her know I'm praying for her? And you—finish that summer reading!

His phone buzzed again.

Nag nag. Almost done. Will tell her.

Jake smiled. He gathered all the materials he'd need for the presentation and started toward the conference room. His phone buzzed.

I miss U.

His heart stopped. That boy. His boy. He typed back.

Miss you, too, bud.

With a grin and a surge of confidence, he got the meeting setup. If these clients didn't sign a contract, it wouldn't be because of anything they'd done.

"WHEN DO we get to meet her?" Gabe propped his feet on the coffee table in the middle of his living room, slipping his arm around his fiancé, Tori's, shoulders as she sat on the couch next to him.

"I thought she was the investigative reporter. What's with all the questions?" Jake slouched low in the arm chair and crossed his ankles.

"He's only asking because I've been peppering him with questions for over a week. I think he's getting tired of not having answers." Tori grinned. "At least, he should be."

Rick and Annabelle came in from the kitchen carrying a plate of cookies, a pitcher of iced tea, and glasses. Annabelle knocked Gabe's feet off the table before arranging the snack.

Jake shrugged. "I don't know. It's complicated."

Rick's eyebrows shot up. "You don't know what?"

"When you'll get to meet Deb. Or even if, frankly." Jake leaned forward and snagged a cookie.

Annabelle glanced up from pouring tea and frowned. "Why is it complicated? Obviously I'm out of the loop."

"Join the crowd." Rick patted the space next to him on the love seat.

"I only have sketchy details." Tori took a glass of tea and a cookie and glared at Gabe. "*Someone* just says it's Jake's story to tell and then clams up."

Jake hunched his shoulders under the weight of their gazes. He outlined the basics with as little detail as possible. What was the point of dragging them all into the middle of it if things never went beyond him having some time with Sean? Given the silence from Deb all week, it seemed like that was what she was angling for. Sean's texts were slightly more optimistic, but he was just a kid. How much would Deb tell him? "I don't know much more than that myself. From what Sean has said, the school board called an emergency meeting and it's likely she'll get the department chair position. But I don't know."

"When are they meeting?" Tori brushed cookie crumbs off her jeans.

"Tonight, I think." Jake shrugged. "Might've been last night. But I really think Sean would've texted me with an outcome."

"They're meeting on a Friday night? That is a special meeting." Tori scoffed. "Last time the school board up here met on any day other than Wednesday I think it was because one of the members died and they had to swear in the temporary replacement."

"She really wants to stay there? After what that guy tried to pull? How do you work for someone like that?" Annabelle shook her head. "I couldn't do it."

"She moved a lot as a kid. She seems to think putting up with that is better than the 'instability' of moving Sean. I don't know, maybe it is? I never moved during high school. But even so, I'd be hard pressed to stick with a job like that for the sole sake of avoiding a move."

Rick took Annabelle's hand in his. "There isn't anywhere else nearby she could teach?"

Jake shook his head. "From what I gather, there's one high school for the county down there. It's pretty rural."

"Too bad they can't move up here. Then you could see Sean

more, and have an easier time wooing his mom." Gabe reached for another cookie.

Tori snorted out a laugh. "Wooing? What century are you from?"

Rick, Annabelle, and Jake laughed.

When his mirth had calmed, Jake sighed. "I'd love it if she came up here. I just don't know how to convince her to do it."

"Pray about it." Rick pressed a kiss to Annabelle's forehead. "God can do some amazing things if we ask."

"Hear, hear." Gabe kissed Tori's cheek.

Jake smiled. It was true. His friends had faced some major obstacles in their own romantic pursuits. And look at them now. Both were happily engaged to women who were clearly the right match for them. Was it possible God had something just as wonderful in store for him? He could only hope.

18

Deb paced from one side of her living room to the other. The school board was meeting tonight in closed session. Who knew that was even something they could do? Didn't they have to keep their proceedings open to the public? Obviously not, but still. The phone call from her dad hadn't given her much hope. Only one of his friends was still on the board after the last election, and the new members didn't seem to have any interest in telling a new principal how to run his school. While maybe not recommended, Peter's actions weren't technically against any regulations. He could choose department chairs. And he could terminate contracts. She'd never joined the teacher's union, and in this case that wasn't working in her favor. Dad had said not to fret, that it could still work out in her favor but she wasn't optimistic.

"Mom, you need to chill." Sean came in from the kitchen with an enormous bowl of cereal. He slurped up a spoonful. "Pacing isn't going to make them decide faster."

She frowned. "Go sit at the table with that. You're going to spill all over everything. Have you finished your summer reading?"

"Geez, Mom." Sean moved to the table and sat. "Almost, okay? And what does it matter if we're gonna have to move? Have you even started looking for a new position yet?"

"We're not moving. I won't do that to you." Deb crossed her arms. She could always get a job in retail somewhere if that's what she had to do. Not that it would pay like teaching did, which was saying something, but she wasn't uprooting them.

Sean jerked one shoulder. "Why not? Could be fun. New town, new faces, new opportunities. Maybe someplace closer to Jake?"

Deb winced. Was that was this was about? "I'll work out a way for you to keep seeing Jake, honey. I promise. We don't have to move up there for that to happen."

"But why stay here if you're not teaching?" He scooped another enormous bite of cereal. "That doesn't make sense. What are you gonna do, work at the grocery store?"

"If I have to. There's nothing wrong with that, it's an honest living." Would it be enough to make ends meet? And the people...as a teacher, she knew so many of the families. She couldn't go anywhere without running into a past or present student or their parents. What would they think when they saw her running a cash register instead? Ugh. But she'd survive. Maybe her pride would suffer, but that wasn't the end of the world.

Sean shook his head. "Whatever."

"What's that supposed to mean?"

"It means if the situation was reversed, you'd tell me to move on. Think about it. Say I had an argument with the captain of the team and he got me kicked off the team, and the coach supported him? Would you tell me to stick it out and bring the other guys water at all the games or would you encourage me to find something else?"

"It's not the same thing at all."

Sean snorted. "Okay."

"Besides. I might not get kicked off the team. We won't know until the school board rules."

Sean picked up his bowl. "I'll be in my room reading."

Was he right? Should she be willing to move? Deb looked around the little house that had been their home for so long. Roots. She'd wanted roots and she'd planted them. And now they were getting ripped up against her will. Could she replant them somewhere else and thrive? And if she took that step, did she owe it to herself to give Jake a chance?

Deb tucked a blanket over her legs and clicked on the TV. Almost midnight and still nothing. They must have adjourned by now. Wouldn't her dad's friend call him so Dad could tell her ahead of the official call? Would they tell her on a Saturday or make her wait? Her prayers had devolved from actual words to pleas for...something. Sean's words had jostled something loose in her heart. Maybe a fresh start wouldn't be so bad. Leaving home—leaving her parents—though. She'd never lived away from them. The thought bordered on terrifying.

She picked up Sean's phone and swiped it on. He charged it in the living room—house rule—and periodically she checked his texts and online activity. He was a good kid, but it never hurt to verify. Her finger hovered over Jake's name. Was that intrusive? Other kids didn't give her a moment's pause but Jake was his father. And a friend. She tapped the message. Reading through their exchanges, her belly quivered. This man cared for her son. And for her.

With a deep breath, Deb set Sean's phone aside and grabbed her own. She'd had a friend in college who moved up near D.C. to teach. What would it hurt to reach out and see if there were any openings? She scrolled through her contacts and typed out a quick email, attaching her resume as an afterthought. Before she could talk herself out of it, she hit send.

She poked Jake's name and composed a text.

Still haven't heard anything. Tomorrow, I guess. Putting out some feelers. Pray for me?

Her finger hovered over send. Should she? She thought of the exchange he'd had with Sean and her heart warmed. Deb pressed the screen.

She turned the TV off. She should go to bed, but she was too wired. So much was up in the air...how were you supposed to function when there were no answers in sight? Her phone chimed.

Already praying. Will continue. Where are you looking?

Deb hit call. If they were both up, there was no point in texting.

"Hey. I didn't want to wake Sean by calling. How are you holding up?"

She gave a mirthless chuckle. "I'm not. I really think high school was the last time I did something impetuous. And we know what happened there. I like order. And plans. And this uncertainty is killing me."

"Want to hear something funny?"

"Sure. Might take my mind off things."

"I dug out my yearbooks. I was trying to see if I could remember you at all. Turns out I had a crush on you."

Oh, sure. "Jake."

"I'm serious. You don't have to believe me, but I can show you my yearbook if you want. Of course, you'd have to come up this way to do that...any chance that might be soon?"

She blew out a breath. So he hadn't moved past his question about where she was looking. "I don't know. I have to see what the school board down here says. I did reach out to a friend up that way. But if things here aren't as bad as I thought..."

"You'd stay? Work with that guy after what he tried to pull?"

"I love my job. I love the kids. This place...it's what I know. I have roots here. I don't really expect you to understand—"

"Whoa there. I do understand. I was happily settled here after college when I got moved overseas. It was expedient for me to go, so I went. I didn't like it, not at first, but that changed quickly. This year, when it was time to come back, it was the same, just in reverse. I've been back here several months and it still doesn't feel like home. But I know it will. This is where God moved me, so it's where I'm going to bloom."

Maybe he did understand. But he didn't have Sean...who wouldn't thank her for using him as an excuse. He wanted to move. Maybe wanted was overstating it, but he wasn't opposed to it. "Thanks. I think maybe I needed to hear that."

"Anytime. Will you let me know what the board says?"

"Yeah." Deb tried to stifle the yawn that snuck up on her, but failed. "I should get to bed."

"Sweet dreams." Jake disconnected the call.

Deb stared at the phone for a moment before plugging it back in. If her dreams continued as they'd been going since camp, they'd be of him. "Yeah. You, too."

"DEBORAH MAGARRY, I cannot believe you emailed me your resume."

Caroline sounded exactly the same as she had in college— like an over-excited cheerleader who was getting ready to do a flip. "Hi, Caroline. How are you?"

"Yeah, whatever. Blah blah niceties. Are you seriously looking for a new job? Up here? 'Cause if so, you are the answer to so many prayers you have no idea."

Deb blinked. "What do you mean?"

Caroline sighed, her breath fuzzing in the phone. "Our

math department is in shambles. The department chair didn't come back last year and the guy who took over...I think, honestly, he just had no idea what was involved. So he turned in his resignation last week. Last week! Teachers report on Monday and right now, my math department is a rudderless ship. There are four other teachers and they're all great, but they've also all made it clear that they're happy to come in, teach math, do whatever club or activity they've always done, and go home. None of them want to be chair. Or teach calculus."

"Calculus? Really?" Deb sat up straighter. She'd been dying to move into more advanced classes, but was always told she was better at the foundational levels. Plus, they rarely had enough interest to offer anything beyond what was required by the state to graduate.

"I've got three full classes. All advanced placement. I have one teacher who is, grudgingly I might add, considering doing one of them. But...I need to know if you're serious."

God, is this You? It was too much. She still hadn't heard from the school board. It was almost noon. But—Calculus! "What else would I teach?"

Papers shuffled in the background. Then there was typing. "Let's see. I have Pre-calculus with Trigonometry—two classes of that, and an Honors Geometry class that need covering."

Deb's heart soared. All her favorites. And department chair to boot? The upper level classes were optional and didn't tend to attract the kids who wanted to argue with you about whether or not they were going to ever use it. Plus, the math itself was beautiful in its complexity and a simple joy to teach. "I'm in."

"Seriously?"

Deb swallowed. Her heart was pounding in her chest...but it felt right. "Yeah. Oh wow. Yeah, I am. What do I need to do?"

Caroline laughed. "I'll shoot you an email with all the details. Expect some calls, today if I can find anyone willing to help me out on a weekend. I guess there's no way you could be here on Monday?"

"I can make it work. I'll probably have to bring Sean, but he's—"

"Not a problem. Bring him. I can't believe this, you're a lifesaver."

"No. Caroline you have no idea. This is God at work." She smiled as her friend whooped. "I'll...see you Monday morning."

"You'll see who Monday morning?" Sean shuffled into the living room rubbing his eyes.

Deb set her cell down on the arm of the couch and considered her son. He'd been adamant that moving wouldn't be the end of the world. It was time to test the waters. "Caroline. You remember her?"

Sean yawned and scratched his head. "Oh, yeah. Sure. I...doesn't she live near D.C.?"

"You said you'd be okay with moving." Deb held her breath. Had he been serious?

He grinned. "Really? Awesome. Hey, can I come?"

"That's the plan. In fact...I should call your grandparents. There's a lot to do." The mental checklist was rapidly growing. Pack. Find an apartment. Get the house on the market. Her parents could handle selling the house. She should get one of those moving trailers delivered. They could pack everything in it and store it 'til they were settled up there. A hotel for the first little while.

"Can I call Jake?"

Her heart stuttered in her chest. Jake. Another person she needed to know was serious about their words. She nodded. "Yeah. Sure."

She was already reaching for her phone when it rang. Her dad. Well. It didn't matter what the school board had decided anymore. She was leaving. There was a leaden ball in her stomach and the barest hint of nausea. "Hi, Dad."

"Hi, hon. Did Greg call you?"

"Not yet. But I don't care what they decided." She took a deep breath. "I'm taking a job in Fairfax."

"They—you're what?"

"I'm taking a job in Fairfax. I reached out to my friend Caroline, and it turns out she's been praying for someone. I'm supposed to be there on Monday when teachers report." Deb's tongue darted between her lips. Why wasn't Daddy saying anything?

After several seconds, he finally spoke. "I'm proud of you, Deborah. I know moving isn't easy for you. But this...feels right."

"It really does. Thanks, Dad."

"Mom and I'll be over with some boxes. Think one of those places that bring trailers over and then move them for you could deliver today?"

She laughed. "You read my mind. I don't know, but I'm about to call and find out."

"What will you do about the house?"

"Sell it. There's that one realtor at church who always seems nice. She's on my list of people to call, too." She needed to start writing the list down or she was going to forget half of it.

"Why don't you let me get Mom on that? I'm pretty sure they're friends. We'll bring lunch when we come. Love you."

"Love you, too."

Deb dropped onto the couch, grabbed a notepad and pen, and started on her list. Dad never did say what the board decided. It didn't matter. She shook her head. Less than twelve hours ago, it would've been the only thing she wanted to know. She added "email resignation" to the list and grinned. Calculus. It might be a bit of a challenge. She hadn't done much of it since school, but it'd come back. With a renewed sense of purpose, she opened a browser on her phone and started in on her to-dos.

19

J ake paced in the vestibule of the small Chinese restaurant across the street from Deb's new school. He hadn't believed it when Sean called him on Saturday, but when Deb texted from their hotel after they arrived Sunday evening...he hadn't slept. They were here and planning to stay.

He'd kicked around telecommuting options with Gabe and Rick on Friday night. They'd had a tentative plan for him to spend Thursday through Monday down near Deb and Sean and then be back in the office on Tuesday and Wednesday. It would have been hectic, and a lot of driving, but worth it. Not just to see Sean, but because of Deb. He ached to see her again.

The door opened and Sean barreled through. "Jake!"

"Hey, man." Jake raised his fist for a bump. "How's the new school look?"

"It's school." Sean shrugged, but his eyes sparkled. "I got my schedule all worked out. The ladies in the front office are nice. They gave me cookies."

"Cookies? Why didn't I hear about cookies?" Deb peeked

around her son. Her eyes met Jake's and electricity sizzled through him. "Hi, Jake."

He grinned and reached for the door into the restaurant. "Hi."

When they were seated in a curved, C-shaped booth with steaming cups of tea and a general consensus of what to order, Jake took a deep breath. This could be his life. Dinner with his family. His *family*. He glanced to where Deb sat on his right and eased his hand toward hers rested on the seat of the booth. Jake let his fingers rest on top of her hand. She jolted, her head swiveling and her gaze locking with his. He swallowed disappointment and yanked his hand back, stopping as her fingers caught his.

Her smile was tentative, but warm.

He was afraid his grin was goofy. Schooling his expression as best he could, he turned to Sean. "What about that summer reading?"

Sean rolled his eyes. "Don't you ever let up?"

Jake shrugged. "Nope."

Sean snorted. "As it turns out, it's pretty much the same as what they assigned here. So I have to finish it anyway, with one substitution."

Deb laughed. "Poor baby."

"Whatever."

"Hey, at least she didn't say 'I told you so.'" Jake chuckled. "What about you, teach?"

"I'm so excited I can hardly stand it. The other math teachers seem really nice and Caroline wasn't exaggerating when she said none of them wanted to be department chair. I worried she was doing a friend a favor and not being completely honest. I think it's going to be a good fit. Of course, I haven't taught any of these classes before so the prep will be heavy for a while, but I'm kind of looking forward to that."

"Sounds exciting. Always good to do something that excites

you. Where are you going to live?" This area wasn't a terrible commute to Arlington. It could definitely be worse. He was getting ahead of himself, but he couldn't seem to stop.

"I thought we'd look for something to rent to start out. I'm committed for a year, and probably beyond that seeing as how Mom and Dad are meeting with a realtor tonight to get our house listed. But I don't know how far housing money goes in the area. I guess I need to find someone up here. For now, we're in an extended stay place down the road. I don't want to be there too long, but it'll do for the time being."

Jake nodded and squeezed her hand. "I'm sure you'll find something soon."

Sean laughed. "Right. You haven't seen how picky mom is."

"I am not."

Jake quirked an eyebrow. She'd certainly been picky at camp.

Deb frowned. "Fine. Maybe I am. But I don't see anything wrong with knowing what you want and not settling for less."

"Speaking of that, what happened with the school board?"

"I didn't even want to find out, but my dad spilled the beans. Ultimately, they made Peter back down on the Department Chair job because of rules in place for when people are eligible for that position. And he's being watched for this first year to see if he tries to circumvent policy in any other way. Even still, I'm not sure how I would've managed if I'd stayed. To go back, knowing that the two of them had been conspiring like that?" Deb shook her head. "This job—this move—was so clearly God at work."

Jake's gaze snapped to hers and held it. "I can't argue with you there."

∾

HE LOOKED around the two bedroom suite at the extended stay hotel. "This is better than I imagined."

She laughed. "I don't want to be here forever, but yeah, it's not so bad. And Sean has his own space so no one gets underfoot."

"Speaking of which, I think I'm gonna go read. 'Night, Jake. 'Night, Mom." Sean hovered for a moment and caught Jake's eye, giving him two thumbs up before disappearing down the small hallway.

Well, at least Sean approved. Did Deb? Jake tucked his hands in his pockets and wandered to the sliding doors that led out onto a tiny concrete patio that looked out over the parking lot. "Have you been out here?"

She shook her head. "It doesn't seem overly sturdy. I mean, what's anchoring that concrete into the wall?"

"Really?" Jake unlatched the door and pulled it open. He stepped out onto the patio and gave a little bounce. "Seems sturdy enough. Come on, it's a nice evening, for August."

"Are you sure? Maybe we should just..."

Jake held out his hand.

Deb pressed her lips together and slowly reached for him. When their fingers were laced, she stepped out onto the tiny rectangle and edged closer to Jake. "I'm not sure about this. I really think they're only supposed to be for decoration."

Jake laughed and slipped his arm around her shoulders, drawing her close to his side. After a moment, her arm slid around his waist. He let out a contented sigh. "See? Not so bad, is it?"

She leaned her head against his shoulder. "Maybe not."

They stood like that for several minutes, the only noise the traffic speeding by and the few crickets that made themselves heard when the cars thinned out.

"I'm glad you're here." Jake shifted so he could hold her gaze. Maybe she'd see and believe the truth of his words.

"Me too."

Slowly, to give her time to evade as much as to be sure she understood his intent, Jake lowered his forehead to hers. "I'm glad you're staying."

She nodded, her breath hitching.

Jake lowered his lips to hers, pulling her closer so their bodies touched. Her hands slid up his arms and clasped around his neck. He held her waist, using all his will not to move his hands and turn the kiss into something more than what they were ready for. He eased back.

"I'm not...I don't know...Jake. What is this?"

"I want to spend time with you, get to know you even more than I did at camp. I want you in my life, not just now, but forever. Not because of Sean. But because you make everything about life brighter and sweeter than it was before. What is this? It's me saying I love you and asking if there's any chance you'll ever love me back." Jake held his breath, his heart hammering in his chest.

"I didn't want this to happen." Deb shook her head and Jake winced. Heat flooded through him and he turned away to stare out over the parked cars. What had he been thinking? He'd promised himself he'd go slow, be cool. And the first opportunity that came up, he tossed his heart on the pavement for her to stomp on.

"Oh."

Deb grabbed his hand as he started for the sliding door. "I used every excuse I could come up with to avoid it. And maybe someone should have told you to be careful what you wish for, because I'm used to doing things my own way and I'm not sure how easily that will change. I'm not sure of a lot of things right now, and that's not a comfortable place for me to be. But in spite of that? I love you, too, Jake."

"Woohoo!"

Jake laughed and turned to see Sean standing in the doorway. "What are you doing there, man? I'm trying to have a moment with your mom."

"I was going to ask if you guys wanted ice cream."

Deb made a shooing motion. "We'll get some later. We have more pressing matters to attend to."

Sean pulled the sliding door closed and disappeared from view. Jake turned to Deb. "We do?"

She nodded.

"What's that?"

"I need you to kiss me again, the way you do that makes the world explode into a kaleidoscope of color."

Jake grinned, his heart soaring as he wrapped his arms around her. "It might take me awhile to get it just right."

Deb slid her arms around his neck and pulled him close. "We have all the time in the world."

A NOTE FROM ELIZABETH...

Wow. Talk about some baggage to work through! But Jake and Deb finally got it figured out. They're on the way to a permanent happy ending, and in the mean time, Sean has his dad back in his life.

The three founders of Intelligence Associates may have found love, but there's still one of their admins in need of a second chance. Both of Shannon's daughters are ready to start school, but the Kindergarten teacher may be more than anyone bargained for.

Read Operation Back to School today!

AUTHOR'S NOTE

Thank you for reading *Operation Fireworks!* I hope that you enjoyed it! I would appreciate it if you'd help others enjoy it too by leaving a review on Amazon, Goodreads, and any other retail site you frequent. Word of mouth is how most people say they find new books to read, so I'd love it if you'd also consider telling your friends about it. Any success my books have is owed to readers like you who take the time to tell others about my stories. Thank you, from the bottom of my heart.

You can always keep up to date with my writing news via my occasional newsletter. There's a sign-up form at my website http://www.ElizabethMaddrey.com and also on my author Facebook page http://www.Facebook.com/ElizabethMaddrey.

I continue to owe a huge debt of gratitude to my husband and sons for giving me the time to write, my sister for her unflinching support and encouragement, and my critique partners Lynellen Perry, Heather Gray and Jan Elder for catching all the times I use the same word six times in two paragraphs.

More than anything, I'm grateful that God continues to give me words and makes it possible for me to write them down.

I'd love to hear from you! You can connect with me on Facebook my webpage or via email.

WANT A FREE BOOK?

If you enjoyed this book and would like to read another of my books for free, you can get a free e-book simply by signing up for my newsletter on my website.

OTHER BOOKS BY ELIZABETH MADDREY

Beachfront Billionaires

Second Chance at the Seaside

Married at the Marina

Billionaire Next Door

The Billionaire's Nanny

The Billionaire's Best Friend

The Billionaire's Secret Crush

The Billionaire's Backup

The Billionaire's Teacher

The Billionaire's Wife

Postcards, A Novel

So You Want to Be a Billionaire

So You Want a Second Chance

So You Love to Hate Your Boss

So You Love Your Best Friend's Sister

So You Have My Secret Baby

So You Need a Fake Relationship

So You Forgot You Love Me

Hope Ranch Series

Hope for Christmas

Hope for Tomorrow

Hope for Love

The 'Grant Us Grace' Series

Wisdom to Know

Courage to Change

Serenity to Accept

Pathway to Peace

Joint Venture

The 'Remnants' Series:

Faith Departed

Hope Deferred

Love Defined

Stand alones

Kinsale Kisses: An Irish Romance

Luna Rosa (part of A Tuscan Legacy)

Her Billionaire Benefactor (part of the Easter in Gilead series)

For the most recent listing of all my books, please visit my website.

ABOUT THE AUTHOR

USA Today bestselling author Elizabeth Maddrey is a semi-reformed computer geek and homeschooling mother of two who lives in the suburbs of Washington D.C. When she isn't writing, Elizabeth is a voracious consumer of books. She loves to write about Christians who struggle through their lives, dealing with sin and receiving God's grace on their way to their own romantic happily ever after.

- facebook.com/ElizabethMaddrey
- instagram.com/ElizabethMaddrey
- amazon.com/Elizabeth-Maddrey/e/B00A11QGME
- bookbub.com/authors/elizabeth-maddrey
- youtube.com/@ElizabethMaddreyAuthor

www.ingramcontent.com/pod-product-compliance
Lightning Source LLC
Chambersburg PA
CBHW071303130626
46556CB00003B/1441